THE WORMWOOD EMAILS

Insider Tips on Avoiding Hell

By R. J. Aldridge

The Wormwood Emails by R. J. Aldridge
Published by R. J. Aldridge

© 2019 R. J. Aldridge

All rights reserved. No portion of this book may be reproduced in any form without permission from the publisher, except as permitted by U.S. copyright law. For permissions contact:

emailwormwood@gmail.com

Cover by R. J. Aldridge

ISBN: 978-1-64516-418-0

To the Memory of C. S. Lewis

The inspiration for this book is clearly taken from The Screwtape Letters, which was first published in 1942. Since that time, millions of people have come to understand the wisdom and clarity that only "Jack" could convey, to Christians as well as those that are just curious about "mere" Christianity.

As to the multitudes of C.S. Lewis fans, please remember to be kind to this imitator of the best Christian apologist the modern world has seen to date.

R.J. Aldridge

Preface

It had been a cold and wet Halloween night, even in Oregon, where cold and wet come naturally in late October. The few Trick or Treaters who had been about earlier had long since returned to their homes to count their booty in dryer surroundings.

A thunderstorm had started shortly before midnight and from the brief time gap between the flash and the rumble, wasn't far afield. At times like that, I wished that I had spent a bit more for a higher quality surge suppressor, rather than the little rocker switch mechanism in the multiple plug extension cord.

I have always enjoyed working late at night, with the house quiet and distractions few. It had been a long day, however, and I still had to complete a software upgrade. When I accidently copied one of those ridiculously long series of letters, numbers and symbols supplied as a License Key into the address bar and not into the registration form itself, my browser dutifully took me to a kind of website that I had never visited before.

From what I've read, there is a hidden "dark web" on the Internet, where sites hide from Google and the other search engines instead of begging to be found by them. They evidently have complicated URL addresses, never meant to be located by people who aren't clued in, so to speak, as to what they are all about and where to locate them.

Personally, I had never gone looking for the dark web, as I knew that the Internet could certainly be depraved enough. Nevertheless, somehow I had stumbled upon what appeared to be a demonic blog site or communications portal. I did some browsing on Cerberus, which was the name of the local search engine option and came across a file labeled "Wormwood".

Now I knew wormwood to be a plant from which a bittering agent has been made for centuries and because of this, the word has

The Wormwood Emails

come to describe something very bitter or harsh. I also vaguely recalled something unpleasant in the Book of Revelation that describes a star by that name falling from the skies and causing mass destruction on earth.

As I started to read, I quickly determined that this file had nothing to do with either astronomy or horticulture. It was rather a series of emails written from one demon, apparently named Wormwood, to another called Wart Hog about techniques to be used in securing human souls for hell. As demons, their ideas about the world are naturally different from our own. For example, God is usually referred to as the "Enemy" and Satan as "Our Father Below". What they see as good we would be more likely see as bad and so on. In general, their view of things is upside down from our own.

As we have only the correspondence from Wormwood and not from Wart Hog, it is a rather one-sided conversation. Perhaps Wart Hog noticed that Wormwood was a bit full of himself and doubted that his own emails in response would be taken seriously anyway. Pride seems to be as much of a problem in hell as it is on earth.

Now I don't know if you believe in demons or not. Even if you do, you might think the idea of a personal tempter targeting your own soul for hell as hyperbole. Or perhaps like the Apostle James, you believe that our own sinful nature presents us with enough encouragement in that direction that a demon to assist simply isn't necessary.

I also have some reservations on the subject. With over seven billion people on the planet, it would seem far too many souls for the demons to work on all at once. At the same time, however, I don't want to place artificial borders around the supernatural. My concept of what would be necessary or rational in our natural world could prove inadequate in the spiritual one.

The Bible tells us bits and pieces of a war in heaven which resulted in the casting out of the archangel who we now call Satan. Not only was he cast out but also a veritable army of angels who supported him were as well. Based on a verse in Revelation, some feel that the number of rebels was as much as one third of the host of angelic beings. Therefore these "fallen angels" are no doubt quite numerous as the description of the angels in heaven being "ten thousand times ten thousand" effectively puts the total beyond counting.

In the book of Matthew, Jesus said in verse 18:10 "See that you do not look down on one of these little ones. For I tell you that their angels in heaven always see the face of my Father in heaven". If children have their own "guardian angels" then could the rest of us not be so blessed as well? After all, Psalm 34:7 says that "The angel of the Lord encamps around those that fear him, and he delivers them". Does not Hebrews 1:14 declare that angels are "ministering spirits sent to serve those who will inherit salvation".

If angels are present, then could demons not be given a similar and counter balancing job assignment? Nothing in red tights with a pitchfork sitting upon your shoulder, but an evil presence of some kind none the less? Perhaps some people are so far advanced in their service to God that the demons have largely given up on them. Or perhaps others have descended so far into evil that they no longer have need of any demonic influences to drag them even further downward. As to the rest of us, could they not share the load, so to speak, only visiting us from time to time when they feel we require their special "ministrations"?

Perhaps my sense of pride doesn't want to admit that there is a part of my character dark enough to be mistaken for something which might come from a devil of hell. In many ways, it is easier to blame our shortcomings on a creature like Wormwood than to admit to ourselves that we can be sinful enough on our own volition.

As you read, you may see (as I did) shades of yourself in Wormwood and in his opinions and advice. Whether such thoughts come from a little devil whispering in one ear or from the moldy

The Wormwood Emails

corners of your own heart, both must be exorcised. In the long run, perhaps the evil tendencies within our own hearts are more formidable than any which could seek to affect us from without?

CHAPTER 1

From: Wormwood <wormwood@gehenna.email>

Sent: Friday, November 30, 2018 4:55 AM

To: Wart Hog <warthog@gehenna.email>

Subject: Introduction

My Dear Wart Hog,

I have heard the humans say on more than one occasion that "two heads are better than one". Having worked on many humans in my time, I rather doubt that this is often the case. Whenever they get together, they seem to make an even greater effort to convince each other that they are something which they clearly are not. Most of them are nothing more that amateur actors, or what the Bible calls hypocrites.

In any case, perhaps the "two heads" approach is the rationale behind the new edict from Low Command that we regularly share information about our respective human patients as well as various strategies for tempting them and eventually securing their souls for Our Father Below. I am not wholly unfamiliar with this approach, as I was once in regular correspondence with an honorary "Uncle" of mine called Screwtape. I'm sure that you could have heard of him, as he is now the infamous Senior Minister for the European Theater of Operations.

During the latest of what the humans naively called "World

R.J. Aldridge

Wars", I was responsible for a young male patient in England. During that time, Uncle Screwtape shared many ideas on ways to procure his soul which proved, as I recall, quite ineffective. Despite this poor advice, I was making solid progress towards acquiring his soul for Our Father Below, when he was most unfortunately translated from the mortal to the spiritual state during one of the periodic bombing attacks occurring in England during that time period. Clearly this was not my fault, as human warfare is a decidedly tricky thing to manage, but none the less the patient slipped from my grasp and I fear the Enemy must have redeemed him.

Many humans I have observed appear to believe that physical death, especially if it comes suddenly to one so young and healthy as my patient was at the time, to be the very worst of all possible evils. I have heard them cry out and even curse against the Enemy, or at least their very limited concept of Him, about how very "unfair" this all is. If they only knew that their deaths, at times anyway, can be a merciful thing. For if the human escapes our grasp and receives permanent residency in heaven, for them death can ultimately be a very good thing indeed. A severe mercy for many of them, I grant you, but mercy none the less to take them home before we have an entire lifetime to work on them.

Although I believe that Uncle Screwtape had planned on absorbing me himself, a shortage of qualified tempters at that time saved me from ending up as an entrée upon his table. After receiving some additional training and various motivational incentives at the House of Correction, I was posted to a position within the North American Theater of Operations. Since that time, I am proud to report, my record has been unblemished, with the souls of all eight of my assignments now safely locked up within Our Father's House. I am also proud to point out that my efforts helped four of them to an early grave via suicide, both directly and indirectly by their lifestyles, well before they had a chance at a true repentance.

The Wormwood Emails

You should also be made aware that I have been chosen to participate in a special pilot program involving the study and possible use of the Enemy's "scriptures", or what the humans call their Bible. You may remember that Our Father Below used some of these sayings himself against the Christ during that disreputable period called the incarnation. Knowledge of the Bible is considered somewhat dangerous, however, so I am being carefully evaluated from time to time to see what impact this may have on my work.

It is widely known that the Bible holds an unknown energy or power, which we must learn to twist to our own advantages. When we are successful in doing so, it will prove its worth whatever the risks involved in the process. I mention this to you now, so that you will not be shocked if I make a reference to that which would, under other circumstances, be considered heretical. Nor, as an aside, to be tempted to forward any of my correspondence to the Infernal Police.

I note from your files that you are newly returning to direct temptation assignments after a millennium or so working in the Ministry of Pain. What a glorious assignment! To be directly involved in the application of such marvelous sensory experiences must have been most fulfilling for you.

You will find some things very different now, when compared to your last assignments during what the humans laughably call the "dark ages". The technology is much advanced and most of the people in the western world live in relative comfort, eat well, travel more rapidly and can amuse themselves with an ever-increasing abundance of devices and diversions. They certainly appear different from your old charges in their rough clothing and crude houses, but I believe you will find them refreshingly the same where it counts, within their essential beings. What the Enemy calls their "hearts" never seems to change, at least not unless the Enemy himself starts working to change them from the inside out.

R.J. Aldridge

I suppose that this may be why the Bible seems to be relevant to them, even today. Many of the Psalms, written over 3,000 years ago, offer better insights into the human character than do their modern psychology textbooks. So please don't be intimidated by the appearance of their relative sophistication because if anything, I have found it even easier now to secure their souls for Our Father Below.

Firstly, the various forms of "communication": i.e. books, magazines, newspapers, movies, television, music and that wonderful font of filth known as the Internet, sends out volumes of thoughts and ideas every hour of every day. Years ago, ideas had to be disseminated through a teacher, minister, writer, parent or other source of authority and instruction. Often, this intermediary entity would alter or edit the message as deemed necessary for the wellbeing of the recipient and to maintain a basic sense of morality. It can be difficult to pollute a mind when there are so many filters in the pipeline.

In today's world, we are usually able to go directly to the mind of the patient. Every day now, the movies and television alone pump out more concepts and suggestions than what a human would have been exposed to in a lifetime a century ago. The Internet, of course, is even a better tool for our cause. In less than five minutes a man can be looking at the kind of pornography which was illegal several decades ago and do this all in the privacy of his own home or office. I am surprised that the humans are so concerned about the purity of their water and air while assuming that the oceans of violence, pornography and hatred on the Internet will not affect them or their cultural climate in any way.

We will discuss how the prevailing culture is now our ally in the war and how the Zeitgeist, or "the spirit of the age" is moving in our direction at an unprecedented speed. What I find welcome but a bit bizarre is that the humans are ever pushing it further in our direction. Just listen for the howls of protest of "intolerance" should any of them suggest a Biblical principal might be at all

The Wormwood Emails

relevant to any social question or issue.

Secondly, the gross materialism of today is not only widespread but also widely admired. Now, more than ever, the value of a man is measured primarily by his income and possessions. When the things which they own fail to give them the satisfactions that they expect, they simply think that the problem can be solved by acquiring more of them. MORE is their mantra, quality and quantity both their goal. Any problems or difficulties are generally viewed as external and never to be seen as within the people themselves.

Lastly, they look to the government or to the scientific community (or both) to solve all problems, whether social or physical. If the poor need to be cared for, then the government "ought to do something", meaning that they should address the situation with handouts or other largesse. If their own irresponsible behavior brings addiction, disease and even death upon them, then the scientific community "ought to invent something" to cure the maladies and prevent their reoccurrence. In short, they have abdicated taking any sort of personal responsibility.

The combination of these elements has helped to render religion irrelevant for most of them and a mere formality for many of those still claiming any kind of interest in the subject. Indeed, I see the day rapidly approaching when the North American Theater of Operations moves into the kind of post Christian society that most of the European Theatre has enjoyed for decades now. If things continue along the pathway they are presently taking, another generation or two should do the trick.

Do write to me with details about your patient, together with his immediate family if he has one, as I have found that successful temptation duties are often group activities for us. As to my situation, my man is a rather difficult case, professing to be a Christian for most of his life. Luckily for me, his religious background has made him a believer in a doctrine which they call "eternal security", or "once saved, always saved". By this they mean that if

13

R.J. Aldridge

a person has entered the Enemy's Camp, they cannot, under any circumstances whatsoever lose that position, or what they call "salvation".

Do you wonder why I call this belief fortunate? I declare it so because such a belief can (and generally does) stunt their spiritual growth by virtue of their complacency. Whatever he feels is irrevocably his possession is more likely to be taken for granted, or even completely ignored.

Personally, I find the whole concept rather difficult to swallow, despite the reference in 2 Corinthians 5:17 which implies that a believer is an entirely "new creation". While I know that they don't lose their salvation with the same frequency as losing their car keys or their tempers, I find it hard to believe that they cannot defect from the Enemy's Camp by their own free will. After all, their scriptures also state that only "those who endure to the end shall be saved".

In any case, we haven't been informed yet by Low Command that it is impossible for them to fall from grace, so to speak, so we must act as if repossession for Our Father Below is still possible, even in those cases where their Christian beliefs appear to be the strongest. It may be true that making him the worst type of Christian possible may not serve to secure his own particular soul for hell, but his sins and hypocrisies may be used to prevent many others from taking that same pathway.

With Worst Regards,

Wormwood

CHAPTER 2

From: Wormwood <wormwood@gehenna.email>

Sent: Friday, February 8, 2019 5:25 AM

To: Wart Hog <warthog@gehenna.email>

Subject: Abortion, Euthanasia and "Quality of Life"

My Dear Wart Hog,

Yes, I am so jealous I could spit! For what do I see in your email but that your man is a resident of Los Angeles. Aesthetically, it is such a marvelous place; done up, as it seems, in almost nothing but shades of brown and gray. Even the sky itself is of these colors on a good day. Ethically, we have firmly entrenched fame and fortune as the prevailing local "gods", while most of the residents feel pride and not shame at whole heartedly pursuing them. Like the human Sinatra, they wish to boast at doing it "my way". More often than not, of course, their way is really our own, but they really do understand so little.

What I find even more fortunate are the sheer masses of humanity packed into the region. Because of this and their incessant traffic jams, having to wait in lines constantly and other such small irritations, you can teach him to view other people that they encounter each day primarily as obstacles to be overcome and not the eternal beings which they are.

When they live closely packed among the millions, it is generally difficult for them to see the unique nature and implicit value of

15

a single human soul. That is to say, to value other people than they themselves, the members of their own family, their close friends and any others that they have chosen to attempt to love. Like Scrooge in that story with such a sad ending, the majority of people in the world appear as nothing more than "surplus population" to them, to be ignored or to be overcome.

I'm frequently astounded that they will sacrifice so very much for their own families and so very little for the rest of mankind. Luckily, neither Dickens or the Enemy's story about the Good Samaritan seems to have made an impression on most of them.

I once heard a human remark that the only things which may be truly eternal in this universe were the words of God and the souls of men. He neglects to mention us and Our Father Below, of course, perhaps believing in the Biblical myth of the Lake of Fire. Nevertheless, at the heart of it he is not far from the truth. We, like the Enemy, know that there is absolutely nothing on this puny and inconsequential planet of theirs that is worth nearly as much as even a single eternal human soul.

Why, I have even heard certain agents of the Enemy suggest that the entire incident of the cross would have been undertaken to save just one of the humans. Even though Christ himself seemed to imply this in the parable of the lost sheep, this is clearly preposterous! We believe they are valuable, of course, but this is probably overstating the Enemy's grace and mercy quite a bit, don't you think?

Nevertheless, Hell requires food and these humans suffice nicely for that purpose. Besides, if the Enemy chooses to love them so much and if they are that valuable to Him, what a marvelous way to cause the Enemy pain, by denying Him of their eternal company?

You would think that after thousands of years of seeing all that people and societies ever accomplish eventually coming to nothing more than fallen down buildings and weather scarred monuments, that they would learn the folly of human achievement as

The Wormwood Emails

the ultimate goal in life. Incredibly, they seem largely blind to this fact. It is a good thing for us that most of them aren't at all familiar with the core message of the Book of Ecclesiastes.

In any case, you will find that this numbers game can work to your distinct advantage towards reducing the value attributed by most of them to human life in all its forms. For example, a short time ago we introduced a concern of a "population explosion" and a subsequent fear of a lack of physical resources to easily provide for them all to assist us in our efforts to both legalize and legitimize abortion and to make it a widely acceptable procedure. We let the humans convince each other that every child should be a "wanted child", thereby reducing the value of a human body (and its eternal soul) to a matter of personal and often changeable opinion on the part of another person.

Often, human infants are inconvenient to the parents for one reason or another; wrong timing, too expensive, aren't married, wrong gender, etc. In times past, they would somehow make the best of it and more often than not, love the child all the more in spite (or perhaps as a result) of the difficulties involved. Now we have taught most of them to simply terminate that growing life within, often with little more concern than might be displayed if they were having cosmetic surgery. Indeed, I have heard that over 95% of all abortions being performed today are ultimately being done for reasons that boil down to nothing more than to avoid parental inconvenience.

If the humans were honest with themselves, they would admit that over the last fifty years, since abortion became more widely available and regularly practiced, that any indication of what constitutes "wanted children" would show the opposite is taking hold; i.e. a dramatic increase in children living in poverty, child neglect, physical and emotional abuses, falling academic performance, etc. The fact that abortion remains popular in spite of the evidences against its efficacy remains one of our greatest triumphs in the current age.

In a similar vein, we have recently introduced the idea in the North American Theater of Operations that only a "high quality life" is worth living. Some may call this idea euthanasia, but I prefer them to use the oxymoron "mercy killing" for this makes it seem like they are somehow doing the victim a favor.

While largely focused on the old and the infirm, I have every hope that it will expand to include those newly born that are exhibiting real or even imaginary defects. From there, it is only a short step to the handicapped or seriously injured adults as well. Who knows, perhaps we can get them to see euthanasia as nothing more than a type of delayed abortion, although "every human a wanted human" seems a bit hard to sell, even to humans.

As Hitler, Lenin, Stalin, Chairman Mao and many other despots have demonstrated through the ages; race, ethnic or national origin, political beliefs, religion, educational background, economic status and many other deciding factors can and will be added to this equation soon enough in order to decide what "quality of life" is enough for the rest of society to allow such life to continue.

I'm amused at the fact that Christianity is sometimes criticized, based upon the fact that over the ages various injustices have been done "in God's name". The period that has come to be known as the Spanish Inquisition comes to mind as an example. Most people who level these criticisms don't know that the victims of these injustices were comparatively few in number. During the Spanish Inquisition, it is believed that less than three hundred were put to death over a period lasting longer than a human century. What far greater atrocities were done by the four heroes of hell listed above! If my math is correct, human deaths reached over a hundred million during their bloody reigns.

Humans seldom seem to realize that the real danger very rarely comes from those who, acting in error on religious principles that they have misinterpreted, attempt to influence others accordingly. No indeed, the real damage to mankind is generally done

The Wormwood Emails

by those in power with no religious principles at all. The fact that Jesus himself would have condemned the Spanish Inquisition should excuse the event from being a blot on Christianity for indeed, it is only a blot on mankind. Hitler, Lenin, Stalin and Mao have none other than themselves to attempt a blame.

At least in the case of abortion, the personal motivation behind the act is generally to preserve the status quo by avoiding the embarrassing, the expensive or the otherwise inconvenient. In the case of euthanasia, however, highly subjective and often changeable cultural and political opinions come into play when deciding who lives and who does not.

In the first case, society looks the other way and calls it a woman's choice. In the latter, society takes to social engineering on a much grander scale. It helps our cause when those making that decision have far less at stake than their patients. Like a large company going through yet another round of job cutting, it gives a whole new meaning to being laid off, or what the English call being "declared redundant".

With Worst Regards,
Wormwood

CHAPTER 3

From: Wormwood <wormwood@gehenna.email>

Sent: Saturday, February 16, 2019 11:00 PM

To: Wart Hog <warthog@gehenna.email>

Subject: Real Idols and False Religions

My Dear Wart Hog,

I must admit to some confusion about your comments on pain. How can something that they hate so much be anything other than bad for the humans and therefore, good for us? You are the expert in this arena, however, having spent more than a thousand years in its various applications. When we get together at our next Infernal Convention, you must explain your position to me in greater detail over some hot hemlock punch.

With respect to your question as to whether I think it preferable to completely steer the client away from religion of any sort, I fear that this seems to be nearly an impossibility at this present time. The Enemy has placed within all humans the desire to worship something and therefore, we find that they are all religious creatures on some level of their being. Surely you have noticed that virtually every culture of mankind from antiquity onwards involves some elements of worship?

In more primitive cultures, the worship involves the deification of something in nature, making the sun, the moon, the stars, et. al. into their "gods". Others invent idols of stone or wood which

20

The Wormwood Emails

serve this role. The question isn't really whether they will worship or not, only what we can induce them into worshiping. It really matters very little to us, so long as it is not worship of the Enemy!

A man named Pascal once wrote something along the lines of; "...there is within the heart of every man a God shaped hole, that He alone can fill". I'm afraid that this appears to be the literal truth. It does seem that the Enemy placed a certain feeling of emptiness within each and every one of them, or at the very least, a sense that things can somehow be much better than they currently are. We can and should attempt to induce them to try to fill in that hole with any number of other imitation gods. If they are truly honest about it though, they will find that only the Enemy Himself will truly suffice, for only He completely fills the unique void of His own design and creation. He is, in a word, the only puzzle piece which fits.

Please don't get me wrong, for many of the things that they can be encouraged to worship aren't like the Enemy at all. Their pursuit of these will be so different from worship in the traditional sense that your human patients will not recognize it for what it really is.

Because of this, the people dedicated to these other types of gods won't go anywhere near a church and if asked, would probably say that they aren't religious at all. Never fear, they are worshiping and sometimes quite fervently doing so, regardless of what they may think they are about.

Materialism as a god comes to mind immediately and surely you have noticed that the humans have a natural bent in that direction anyway. They can be made to think for many years (and sometimes for a lifetime) that houses, cars, boats, clothes, bank accounts, etc. can be a source of true and lasting satisfaction. The amusing thing is that regardless of what they acquire, they will never be truly and completely happy; at least, not because of anything material which they possess. For you see, it is axiomatic that they will always want for more and more of what they have, regardless of how much they can accumulate. More often than not, the acquisition of material things ends as a source of frustration and not fulfillment. Someone is said to have once asked a very wealthy and elderly human "how much money was enough" and he is reported to have replied, "just a little bit more than what you have now". This speaks volumes about their natures. If they dedicate their lives to amassing things to own in this temporary physical world, the odds are in our favor that they will end up as the possessions of Our Father Below in the eternal spiritual state.

Another advantage in trying to satisfy their inherent religious bent by the pursuit of the material is that they will likely sacrifice the good things of the present on the altar of what they think the future may hold for them. For example, men in particular can be induced to work far too many hours, always seeking more and more income or prestige, while their children grow up without them and they drift further and further from their wives. Convinced that they are somehow "doing it for the family", they will someday wake up to the fact that the family they had in mind doesn't exist any longer or was largely fictional in the first place.

Instead of (or in addition to) the pursuit of the material, many can be led to try to fill this God shaped hole by the pursuit of various sensory experiences, such as food and drink, sex in its various permutations, sports and other recreational pursuits, expensive vacations, etc. Others may effectively try to plug the gap themselves by concentrating on what they see as their inherent value. These will seek fulfillment by virtue of their physical beauty, education, intelligence, artistic talents, fitness or social standing. The things that you can offer to entice them try to fill the empty spot inside, which was designed for the Enemy and the Enemy alone, can be as varied as your imagination and their willingness to continue onwards with what was always a fool's errand.

Keep in mind that this sense of disquiet that the God shaped hole affords really works as a kind of homing device for them. If they

The Wormwood Emails

were honest, they would keep on the quest right through and past the diversions that we offer until they came to Him, the one and only ultimate source of fulfillment. Our job is to keep them tied up in one or more of the alternative pursuits of satisfaction which we direct them to and never to let them get around to looking for the Enemy.

Remember that when they grow disillusioned with any one of the activities in particular, you need to substitute another as quickly as possible. If you cannot keep them smugly self-satisfied for all of their lives in their wealth, beauty, intelligence, influence, etc. then at least make the transitions to other pursuits rapid and as seamless as possible. It is at these transition points when they are most likely to seek the Enemy's peace.

You may protest that these are not, by definition at least, inherently sinful things in themselves. Stated simply, that is often quite true. Remember that all we need to do to take these pursuits up to the level of sinfulness is simply to exalt them to a stature in the human's life that is reserved for the Enemy alone. In this respect, these things are really no different from any other idol.

It would be nice if we could assist them into Our Father's House without letting them have any positive or pleasurable experiences at all in the process, but that is not the point of the exercise. Our goal is simply to secure their eternal souls in any way we are able, by virtue of the temporal.

There are other areas where the sin comes easier, of course, such as in the overconsumption of alcohol and drugs, but I find that the humans often resort to these as an anodyne against the pain when other pursuits have failed to satisfy them. The Enemy offers happiness as a byproduct of their relationship with Him. The best we can offer is an analgesic when they pursue their own means to fill the void meant for His own presence.

The other things will always fail them of course, because the hole in their hearts can only be filled by the Enemy. Until they turn to Him, they are essentially pouring sand into a funnel. No matter

R.J. Aldridge

how quickly they pour it into the top to temporarily fill up the hollow feeling inside, the hole in the bottom spills it all out as quickly as the top half of an hourglass.

But by all means, if he seems to take on an interest in religious things and if you cannot induce him to worship Our Father Below directly (or at least not do so as yet), then try to steer him towards one or more of the innocuous religions. Whatever you do, don't ever let him ask whether what he hears is "true" but rather, what tickles his intellect or his vanity.

Many humans can be led into an ill-defined faith in some way or another as to a kind of "force" in the universe. A pantheistic belief in a power flowing in and through everything (especially themselves) usually appeals to them. Such a god won't put your patient into much danger of running into anything like the Enemy, who is as personal as He is transcendent. He can commune with the "force" which he imagines, which is anything and everything that he wants it to be, to his heart's content as far as we are concerned. Let him try to tap into it for his own advancements, then you can combine his spiritual beliefs with materialism and some of the other pursuits I have mentioned previously.

Thanks to the efforts of our fellow demons in the Bureau of Counterfeit Religions, there are literally dozens of other alternatives into which you can steer his interests. Islam, Hinduism, Buddhism, Taoism, Shintoism, and any other "ism" you want... just keep him away from Christianity!

With Worst Regards,
Wormwood

CHAPTER 4

From: Wormwood <wormwood@gehenna.email>

Sent: Sunday, February 24, 2019 3:18 AM

To: Wart Hog <warthog@gehenna.email>

Subject: Cosmology and Creation

My Dear Wart Hog,

Yes, I also sometimes find it amazing that the humans can seem to ignore the evidences around them pointing towards highly intelligent design. In Psalm 19, the Bible says that "the heavens declare the glory of God and the skies proclaim the work of his hands". Luckily for us, not many appear to be listening. Perhaps they are all watching television?

You obviously remember from your prior assignments that the humans believed that someone or something had caused the universe, the world and the myriad of creatures that inhabit it to come into being. Even in those days, when they were relatively ignorant about the amazing complexities present within the workings of every living organism, they saw that there had to have been intelligence and energy behind it all.

You may recall that for many generations, the humans thought that the stars numbered just a few thousand or so. Why think otherwise, for this was what they might be able to count on a clear summer's night. We were able to take this "fact" and raise some interesting questions in their minds about the apparent

25

R.J. Aldridge

disparities in Genesis. After all, the Enemy said to Abraham several times that his descendants would be like the "sand of the seashore" as well as like the "stars of the sky". While obviously the sand of the seashore cannot be numbered, everyone believed that the stars were not nearly so numerous. Since the days of the human Galileo, however, their knowledge and understanding of those heavens has continued to increase along with more powerful and sophisticated telescopes and other instrumentation. They now know that the universe consists of billions of individual galaxies and that these galaxies each contain an almost innumerable number of stars. What they call the Milky Way, containing the earth itself, contains more than five billion stars other than their own sun and it is but one of billions of other galaxies.

You might think that this would be a problem for us, as it rather obviously shows that the writer of Genesis knew something about the size of the universe thousands of years before the telescope arrived on the scene. For beings other than humans, it might have been so, but I'm sure that you have also noticed that most men are incredibly obtuse. Truth be told, the majority of the physicists, astronomers, cosmologists and other scientists are no exception to this, in spite or perhaps because of the number of academic degrees which they hold.

I'm glad that it seems fairly universal among the humans that when they discover how something works from what I would call a mechanical point of view, they also seem to lose their sense of wonder as to both the why it is so designed and more importantly for us, the who of the designer. Why this is, we aren't quite sure. Perhaps it is something akin to their tendencies to be less excited about nearly anything once that something actually arrives rather than their excitation about the same thing when it is merely anticipated. In any case, we need to take full advantage of this characteristic at every opportunity.

So, we keep the astronomers busy counting, naming and ranking the celestial bodies; measuring their brightness, distances

The Wormwood Emails

and speed and then arguing amongst themselves about who discovered what and what that all really means. This allows us to keep most of them far too busy to ever give much thought as to what or who has sufficient power and intelligence to set them in order in the first place. If they do give it any thought, let them think like the deists that it is a cosmic force of some sort and leave it at that. That this force is a personal God who not only exists and invites them to know Him further is something which we should never let them suspect.

As an example of how this works, in recent years these same scientists have discovered a number of physical properties of the universe that they have termed "anthropomorphic" in nature, meaning that they appear to be directly designed within very narrow margins to foster and maintain human life. If gravity were a bit stronger, if the so called weak nuclear binding force a bit less, if the earth were a bit closer to or farther from the sun, or any small variations were present in literally dozens and dozens of other physical phenomena, then life as they know it could either not begin at all or could not be sustained once it had started.

Once again, we have managed to get them bogged down in the particulars and in the measurements as to just how finely these lines are drawn. Many of these factors have tolerances of well under 1/10th of 1%, making it highly improbable that they all occurred at the same time through nothing more than chance. Instead of being amazed at this impossible coincidence and giving serious consideration to the possibility of an intelligent Creator, it is relatively easy to get them to argue incessantly about fractions of a percent on the probability scale, proving once again their old adage that they cannot see the forest for the trees.

If your patient has a mind towards these sciences and if you are clever enough, you can actually use this type of information against the Enemy. Simply remind him that as far as he knows, the only life in this vast universe is here on earth and that the earth is a very small thing indeed in the cosmic scheme of things.

R.J. Aldridge

Point out to him that the vast expanse of the universe seems to be nothing but emptiness and cold darkness and he can be induced to take this as an argument for life as "accident" (and if accidental then by correlation, relatively worthless as well). Life is indeed much rarer than their proverb about the needle in the haystack; rather like a needle in a vast field of haystacks or even in a whole world of haystacks stacked three layers high. Have him focus on the commonness of the hay, not the wonder of the needle.

You and I see the vastness of the universe for what it is; namely, as an expression of the characteristics of the Enemy as displayed throughout the material world of His creation. Why indeed does He populate even this small planet with such a wide diversity of all forms of life, if He is not showing forth His qualities? Why so many birds, beetles and butterflies? It is almost enough to make even me believe the Biblical hyperbole of His infinite power, intelligence and creativity.

That God would choose to fill the sky with so many stars, apparently for little more than as a type of example of His glory and as a small indication of His power should be something that fills your man with incredible awe and wonder, even when filtered through the rather limited powers of human comprehension. Play your cards right, however, and he is just as likely to view the whole thing as no more than a tremendous waste of resources!

With Worst Regards,
Wormwood

CHAPTER 5

From: Wormwood <wormwood@gehenna.email>

Sent: Saturday, March 2, 2019 4:23 AM

To: Wart Hog <warthog@gehenna.email>

Subject: The Evolution Distraction

My Dear Wart Hog,

No, even if your patient has no interest in astronomy, I don't believe that this means that you should completely ignore the evidences of an intelligent Designer as they appear in the world around him. As I thought I had said before, this "argument by design" has been advanced for many years as evidence for the existence of one or more gods and thereby still holds some danger of awakening him to that possibility.

In fact, several centuries ago a human named Paley made an interesting analogy to a time piece, now known as the "watch maker argument", which has caused us certain difficulties. Essentially, he stated that if you found a watch lying in an open field, you would not think that it somehow got there all by itself, so to speak. You would notice that it exhibits complexity of design as represented by a number of smaller systems all working together in harmony towards a common goal. You might also postulate that it must have a kind of force or energy that allows it to fulfill its purposes. Such complexity and energy require a watchmaker and could not logically be a product of natural forces operating through nothing but blind chance. He argued that when you also

29

R.J. Aldridge

find much more complex operations present within living organisms, these are strong evidences for Watchmakers of their own.

Luckily, we assisted a chap by the name of Darwin to popularized certain beliefs widely held today that have eliminated the need for any such original watchmaker. In passing, may I say that my sense of the ironic delights in the fact that Darwin was the son of a minister and a ministerial student himself at one point in his life. It adds a certain panache to use such an implement to assist in the snaring of what today amounts to countless human souls.

Over the last hundred years or so, we have succeeded to elevate Darwin's somewhat limited thoughts on change in living organisms and how those changes may apply to the origins of species into nothing less than the (capitals intended) Theory of Evolution. Even though it is still officially a "theory", rest assured that among most scientists it is considered proven fact and certain dogma.

This is interesting, not only because evolution cannot by definition be "proven" but also because the majority of the information discovered by scientists this century has largely disproven Darwin's theory, or at least reduced the probability that it could have occurred to near zero. Keep your patient away from such books as Deaton's "Evolution: A Theory in Crisis" and Johnson's "Darwin on Trial". Remember how the big lie affects people, that what is repeated often enough as being factual is assumed to be just that, particularly when it is declared to be so in the print of expensive textbooks or by those in authority, such as teachers or scientists.

Of course, even evolutionary doctrine doesn't answer the question as to how the universe got going in the first place but just purports to explain how life on earth was supposed to have advanced in both diversity and complexity after those beginnings. If your patient can have faith in evolution to answer the question of change within living organisms, however, it is a comparatively small matter to allow him to think that cosmologists

The Wormwood Emails

must understand how the earth and the universe itself got started as well. In fact, he would likely be quite astounded to know the extent of what they do not understand.

There have been some troubling articles in the human press lately about the so called Big Bang, which seems to give evidences that the universe itself is not eternal and that space, matter and time all had a beginning (perhaps in the same event). Don't let him dwell too much on that, for anything that had a beginning logically had a Beginner as well.

Keep in mind my comments in the last email about how you can keep the humans fascinated by the how of things, without them giving much thought as to the who or the whys. This is almost universally true of them in all fields of study. Take physicians, for example, who know so much about the workings of the human body. They often begin to take that body for granted, although they have only the slightest inklings as to how the majority of these systems actually function. Try asking any of them to fully explain how the brain and nervous system work, or details as to the miracle of a child growing in the womb.

Similarly, each of the scientific disciplines can be focused back upon itself to a remarkable degree. They can even begin to take pride in the small fraction of understanding that they are able to glean, rather than humbleness at what they fail to understand. Rather like a first grader thinking that a computer is a fairly simply thing, because he knows how to turn it on and can successfully push a few buttons and drag the mouse about.

Speaking of mice, the human Longfellow said something like "a mouse should be miracle enough to convert a horde of infidels". He was right, of course, but luckily for us, we are dealing with humans who consider themselves far more sophisticated and therefore much less easily impressed than would the infidels.

With Worst Regards,
Wormwood

CHAPTER 6

From: Wormwood <wormwood@gehenna.email>

Sent: Wednesday, March 27, 2019 11:11 PM

To: Wart Hog <warthog@gehenna.email>

Subject: Lust but Not Love

My Dear Wart Hog,

I note with interest that your patient is unmarried and in his mid-twenties. He is also I assume, a suitable marriage partner by the human's somewhat limited standards of evaluation in such matters?

If this is the case, you will want to give some careful thought about when you wish to encourage him towards marriage. Files at Headquarters will no doubt indicate quite a few females within his sphere that would make excellent choices, virtually assuring that we will secure both of their souls for Our Father Below at the end. In the meantime, there are definite benefits in keeping him unmarried for the time being as a means of subverting him and harming others. I am referring, of course, to his sex life.

He is sexually active, I imagine, although I dare say like most men of his age, not nearly as active as he fancies he would like to be. With the progress that we have made in the media, the Internet and other influencers of human society, he would be quite the rarity if he were not.

The Wormwood Emails

Personally, I think that the battle over sex has been largely won. Many see it as nothing more than any other "natural" biological function, on a par with eating or elimination. What a triumph it has been to take something that the Enemy looks upon with such importance and to trivialize it so! To help them along, we have assisted in saturating television, movies, magazines, books, the internet and rock music with sex and sexual themes ad infinitum. If you like the looks of someone, just "swipe right".

As those who control these mediums continue to tout sex for nothing more than the sake of it, they throw gasoline on an already blazing fire. At the same time, earlier puberty and later average ages for marriage have made the period longer in which we can

do our best work. I find it amusing that people seem surprised somehow by the increases in illegitimacy, abortion and sexually transmitted diseases. Given the advantages that we have in human society today, I would be shocked if we were not doing very well indeed.

Pornography is growing increasingly available and increasingly explicit. I am happy to say that much of it falls into the hands of young men and boys who are least likely to see it for the perversion of reality that it generally is. I notice that an estimated one half of the inquiries on certain computer information networks are requests for one form or another of pornography or for purposes of explicit talk about sex.

Homosexuality seems to be increasing, although not as rapidly as many believe and not so fast as the practicing homosexuals imply. What a sea change that is, by the way, that they boast of their numbers in an effort to gain legitimacy and political clout. Even better, they demand not just passive acceptance of their sexual practices, but that others embrace them as perfectly normal and on a par with heterosexual behaviors. When people resist their demands in this area, we have them shout "homophobia" and have the laws, courts and public opinion force their will

33

upon the rest of society.

I take delight in the irony that the greatest supporters of homosexual behavior are usually those who disbelieve in the Enemy and as such, look to Darwin's theories about "survival of the fittest" for further progress of mankind. Since homosexuals produce no offspring, if it were up to the process of natural selection, they wouldn't make the first cut.

Try to get your man involved in sex to an obsessive degree. He already looks at most young women that he encounters with that activity in mind. Teach him to look at it as the defining factor as to their worth as individuals. If he can be steered to approach each potential relationship with this attitude, the damage to himself and to the young women that he shares a bed with can be enormous.

It is a pity that AIDS and twenty plus forms of venereal disease have helped to rein in a bit of the sexual excesses of the past thirty years. There is some evidence, however, that so called "safe sex" is losing its grip on those who are (or would like to be) promiscuous. No longer the cause of the hour, they fail to remember that the risks remain even when the publicity has faded.

It would appear that the Enemy designed sex for three primary purposes; bonding, procreation and enjoyment. Modern men ignore the first, try to prevent the second and pursue the third with a vengeance. Whether they admit it or not, however, bonding is involved. Every time a man lies with a woman, a certain emotional and spiritual something occurs. It is often felt more strongly by the woman, of course, as they are almost always more sensitive to their emotional side. None the less, the relationship is distinctly more than merely a transient physical one.

When a couple remain married for a lifetime, those sexual acts, though less frequent than in their youth, continue to bind. Over the course of years and the hundreds or thousands of intimate moments shared between them, the "cement" gets very strong indeed. It can take them quite out of themselves, making not only

The Wormwood Emails

the sexual, but their entire relationship into the kind of mutual giving and concern that the Enemy's scriptures advocate and we so despise.

If we can keep sex outside of marriage, however, the forming and tearing that occurs, in all of its various degrees, will make any marriage that the patient enters into later more difficult to maintain. These humans seem to operate a bit like pieces of adhesive tape. The more often you try to make them "stick" to something, the less likely you are to obtain a permanently strong bond when such a bond is finally desired. Your patient probably hasn't noticed, but couples who live together before marriage are less likely to have happy marriages and more likely to eventually divorce. The lack of commitment to the relationship is what caused them to cohabitate, rather than to marry, at the start. In many cases, the commitment doesn't appear just because they decide to legitimize the arrangement.

Do all that you can to get him involved in pornography. Start with movies and other things generally considered harmless by today's society such as "hard R" rated movies, novels, such periodicals as *Playboy* and other "men's magazines". Why, even spending too much time studying the mail order lingerie catalog can be a start. Tell him that he is merely developing an appreciation of literature, film techniques or merely the beauty of the female form. Perhaps you can convince him that sex is really not much more than just another spectator sport?

What is likely to happen is that he will soon tire of the lingerie on the models and wish to see more of the models themselves. Then he will tire of admiring the beautiful centerfolds and hunger for something more "exciting". The next step will be couples, then groups, etc. as he descends into the increasingly explicit, degrading and violent. Soon he will find himself caught up in something far removed from the normal sexual relationship designed by the Enemy for marriage.

The formula is simple, really, and it is basically the same whether

R.J. Aldridge

the sin involves sex, drugs, alcohol, etc. He will find that he needs ever increasing stimulation to produce the same "thrill". What you seek is to produce a constantly increasing craving for a pleasure that is steadily being reduced.

This will damage his views on sex, of course, as he begins to think things normal that are far from it. It will also make a successful and lasting relationship with any one woman very difficult for him, as he will consciously or unconsciously be comparing her to the women of his fantasies. If the real woman in his life does not act the same during their sexual encounters, he may be tempted to find someone who will (he had better look for someone with some acting experience).

In terms of their physical appearance, his wife will likely fall short in one or more areas. It may well be that the potential of the beauty of the stranger may call him away from the beauties of the one that he knows so well. Even if his wife is particularly attractive, by the way, she will get older and less attractive over time. She may compare very well with Miss November of this year, but probably won't hold a candle to Miss November of thirty years hence.

If he does get involved sexually, by all means try to steer him into relationships where there is no emotional attachment. You will enjoy the fact that sex without emotion loses much, if not all, of the joy that can otherwise imbue it. Yes indeed, human sex can and often will become the final refuge of the truly miserable.

With Worst Regards,
Wormwood

CHAPTER 7

From: Wormwood <wormwood@gehenna.email>

Sent: Monday, May 13, 2019 5:49 AM

To: Wart Hog <warthog@gehenna.email>

Subject: "Other" Religions Redux

My Dear Wart Hog,

No you idiot, I am not advocating religion. I'm merely pointing out that if you cannot ensnare your patient with materialism, sensualism, egotism, etc. as his undeclared religion, then you had better steer him towards one of the relatively innocuous religions that we have been able to assist in getting started and helped to grow over the years.

Yes, all religions are likely to have some element of truth in them and are therefore dangerous to us. Remember, though, that only by having some truth can we serve up the false as real. After all, if you were counterfeiting a hundred dollar note, you would not have a small child draw a picture of one with his crayons. Remember, the closer the counterfeit is to the genuine article, the better the deception will become.

As in all things religious, however, we cannot afford to get very close to the truth of the Enemy or of His Christianity. To do so runs the very real risk that the man will awaken to Him and we will be undone. What good are our efforts towards manmade conventions and hypocrisies if the patient ultimately knows the

37

R.J. Aldridge

Truth and it really does "set him free"?

The general rule is to start as far as possible from Christianity and only move, by slow and tiny steps, closer to the real Church if and when you are required to do so. Such an action should only be taken to prevent him from making the jump himself and taking the initiative to walk into an evangelical church someday of his own accord.

I would suggest that you start with something vague, like the New Age beliefs that we know to be as old as mankind itself. These allow for a person to believe virtually anything they wish about anything at all; from auras to crystal power, reincarnation to channeling, astrology to extra-terrestrials, it makes little difference. Although they don't say so in so many words, what they are advocating is a kind of "faith in faith itself". They seem to feel that it doesn't matter what you believe, as long as you are very sincere about it. Ludicrous, I know, to think that crystals and other claptrap can alter the physical, let alone the spiritual realms, but better to leave them be in their ignorance and contrivances.

If your patient is not so great a fool as this, introduce him to the Eastern religions, which have many of the same trappings but are dressed in greater respectability. This may be ascribed to the length of time that we have been able to use them for deceptive purposes, or perhaps because of the large number of people that we have been able to maintain as practitioners of these faiths. In any case, many of these "isms" offer a certain amount of credibility due to the patronage of certain of the rich and famous devotees and therefore even some stylishness as well.

Once again, it matters little to us, as long as this lessens somewhat the search to fill the "God shaped hole" which I wrote about previously. To keep them off track, you will often find that the guise of some type of religion will prove necessary and sometimes even desirable.

If you need something more western, try for one of what true

The Wormwood Emails

believers call the "cults"; the Mormons, Scientologists, Jehovah's Witnesses, Christian Scientists, etc. There are elements of truths in their faiths, to be sure, but they are well hidden. As to the essentials, they are unlikely to lead your man to the Enemy.

Take the Latter Day Saints as an example. Their emphasis on the family and on self-reliance is attractive to many. While they freely acknowledge the Enemy, they also declare that He is only one of a thousands of similar gods and that His divinity, as far as it goes in their doctrines, was achieved. One of their early prophets, Brigham Young by name, said that "As man is now, God once was. As He is now, we may become".

It sometimes surprises me at how little they have changed over the ages. We actually have many of them believing that they can be like God, recycling with great success the same story that Our Father Below told Eve in the garden many thousands of years ago. Then again, why should we change a winning formula? It worked then and it still can work today. Simple and direct appeals to their ego often do so.

If you have to let him get close to more traditional beliefs, I would suggest some of the mainline denominations. It is heartening to look at a country like England that produced so many great theologians, preachers, missionaries and warriors for the Enemy for so many years. Today, only about one in twenty adults in that country ever bother to attend church at all. Those who do go are usually at the Church of England or some such place where often the minister himself could hardly qualify as a true believer in the Enemy. There is little danger for us there.

It can be rather wonderful! The humans in attendance can have the some of the comfort of religion, without the risk of conversion. They can attend services in such a church for months, years or even a lifetime, without a word about sinfulness and the need for repentance being voiced. Let them enjoy looking at the grand old buildings in the frame of mind of an architect or a historian. Let them enjoy listening to the music in the spirit of the concert

39

goer. Let them enjoy the pleasant homilies from the pulpit as he might listen to a favorite story teller or a motivational speaker. Let them even think that they are being "spiritual" in doing any or all of the above. So be it... just don't ever allow them to draw near to the Enemy and to His holiness!

In an effort to remain popular with the masses and simplify doctrines that at times seem difficult to them, churches of this type have largely gutted the truth out of the scriptures. When you take out the truth, however, the power inherent in the truth leaves as well. Usually, the people aren't far behind. Why waste time at a church that isn't any different from the local meeting hall? Why mouth the words in a prayer, when few believe that there is a Listener?

It is dangerous, I know, to let them get so close to the Enemy. We always run the risk that a minister will take over the pulpit who still believes the truth of the scriptures and is willing and able to declare the Enemy's truth effectively. Or, the patient may actually get into a conversation about his beliefs with someone in the congregation who still remembers what it is really all about. In cases such as these, your client may be drawn to reconsider if his formalized ritual is truly all that the Enemy offers or desires.

But remember also that the best place to hide an object is often among things that are something like it. Sometimes the best place to place a human and to win his soul for Our Father Below is in a church, or at least in a church of this type. Yes, I have often found that the "wide road that leads to destruction" can lead through the pews and even through the pulpit as well. Sitting in a church doesn't make one a Christian, just as sitting in a college classroom doesn't make one into a philosopher.

Remember, the word religion comes from the Latin phrase "to reattach" and is largely based upon man's effort to make himself appealing to God upon his own (rather than upon His) terms. The Enemy reaches down in love and grace, He isn't lassoed and then tethered from below.

With Worst Regards,
Wormwood

CHAPTER 8

From: Wormwood <wormwood@gehenna.email>

Sent: Saturday, May 18, 2019 4:43 AM

To: Wart Hog <warthog@gehenna.email>

Subject: You Idiot

My Dear Wart Hog,

What can I say other than that you were a complete fool? Alas, you have probably already figured this out on your own. Why, in the name of all that is unholy, would you allow him to go and listen to an evangelist with the last name of Graham? Yes, I realize that it wasn't quite that simple and once on his way, the Enemy's agents frustrated your intentions to sidetrack him. But really, you should never have let it reach that point.

Although Franklin Graham isn't quite as formidable as his father was, the man who used the rather silly name of "Billy". We tempters in the American Theater have long referred to his father as William the Conqueror. While Franklin hasn't yet grown to the stature of his progenitor, he is still somewhat intimidating.

In spite of years and years of our best efforts, we weren't able to assist Billy into the kind of sins that would serve to discredit his message. We put a number of our finest tempters on the case but as far as I have heard, they have come up quite empty; with no sexual immorality, greed, misuse of money, inordinate pride, etc. As you know, these and other sins have often been used to bring

The Wormwood Emails

down many other humans that threaten us by virtue of their successful and highly visible Christian ministries.

We were gladdened to hear about the elder Mr. Graham passing away and heading to the Enemy's Camp. Hopefully our collective efforts on the younger Mr. Graham will bear more fruit.

I suppose that your man was probably curious about all the commotion that surrounds the name of Graham when one of them comes to a city for one of his rallies. Perhaps he really did mean it when he accepted the invitation of one of his co-workers to attend such a meeting due to simple curiosity. You probably were pleased with the inherent pride and rather superior smugness behind that statement, the feeling of being somehow intellectually superior to those who were going because they actually believed in "that sort of thing".

Too late, I fear, you realized your massive tactical error when you saw him leave his seat and walk forward to accept Jesus as Savior. Next time, please remember that anything at all, including sin itself, that serves to move a man into the Enemy's sphere of influence is dangerous to us and to be avoided at all costs. Short term gains as to pride and religious skepticism really aren't worth that kind of risk in terms of the potential losses.

Well, enough on that for now, for I doubt that you will make the same mistake again in the future. None the less, the problem remains as to what you should do now to mitigate this disaster.

Before you despair too greatly, remember that he may not really be a Christian after all. Thousands of such "converts" walk the aisle because of nothing more than the emotionalism of the moment and/or the peer pressure of hundreds like themselves taking the same journey. Unless he truly is convinced of his own personal sinfulness, looks to Jesus Christ as his only hope for salvation from those sins and has freely and unreservedly surrendered his life to the Enemy, he is probably mistaken as to believing that he is "saved". I think you would be surprised at how many people sitting in church pews each Sunday aren't Christians at all and

43

R.J. Aldridge

hopefully, they will be even more surprised when they join us someday in Our Father's House below.

As to your patient, he will no doubt be looking for a church now, feeling like he really "should" attend one. What you need to make your primary task is to keep him from a church which will provide him with real spiritual nourishment or challenge the depth and sincerity of his convictions. If we can get him into a spiritually dead environment, this short-term affiliation with the Enemy can likely be undone. Indeed, it can often be turned to our favor, as he emerges from a "religions phase" and considers himself a more complete man for having had the experience (and thereby more immune from a similar attack in the future). You know what they say these days... "been there, done that".

At this point, I would suggest that you encourage him to church shop. He will already be inclined in that direction, of course, since consumerism plays such a large part in his life and he is quite used to shopping for other things. The trick is to induce him to approach the "which church" question with criteria similar to what he would apply for a "which car" decision. To look at life as a consumer or user comes naturally for him, so this should not be too terribly difficult to accomplish.

Start by planting the thought, "Yes, but which church is the best one?". Your patient lives in a large city, with literally hundreds of various types of church buildings within easy commuting range. If you can have him spend one or two weeks at each of them, with time off between Sunday visits for golf, trips to the beach and other more important activities, it will take years for him to get around to them all. With any luck at all, your man will move to another geographic region in the meantime and you can start the process all over again.

Being human and therefore prone to judgments based upon the outside appearances, the first thing that he will consider is the look of the church building itself. Never mind that the Enemy has made it quite clear that the Church is composed of the believers

The Wormwood Emails

themselves and not the building that they worship in, for he doesn't really understand this yet. Many of the stalest and God-less churches in the world have very attractive buildings, so try to steer him into one of these. Perhaps he can be fooled into thinking that nice stained-glass windows and aged oak pews are really necessary for a satisfactory worship experience?

Remember, try to keep your patient's focus not on the rather large common area of belief as embodied in the statement of faith of each church, but rather on the differences in the form, style and methodology evidenced in their worship services. Done correctly, the patient will absorb very little of the message of Christianity as you divert his attention to the building layout, the way the services are conducted, the clothing worn, formality of language used, type of music and singing, ordinances, etc.

Once you have him shopping and if it proves possible, try to move your man into the role of a church critic. You know what I mean. Pastor A is "too young" while Pastor B is "too old". Rev. C's preaching is "too casual", while Rev. D's is "too boring". Church A is "too stand offish" and Church B is "too aggressive". Church C is "too old fashioned" while Church D is "too progressive". One of the American presidents, Abraham Lincoln, is reported to have said that "Whether you look for the good or the bad in people, you'll surely find it". Going into each church looking for the negatives is the frame of mind we want to encourage. Never let him think that since he himself and indeed, all people have faults, it makes perfect sense that any particular church with a collection of people attending will undoubtedly experience similar shortcomings.

Remember that by encouraging your patient to shop around for churches, he is unlikely to become very involved with a single local congregation. Therefore, he is unlikely to ever experience anything of the mutual concern and unconditional acceptance which they call "Christian fellowship". Of course, what is also important is that he will not have an opportunity to give of himself to the others. Both failures will most assuredly stunt his growth

R.J. Aldridge

in Christianity. Rather than joining with them and volunteering to help to meet needs and to work to correct any deficiencies that really may be present, he will instead spend his time and energies in digging up and criticizing their faults.

Remember, that humans are highly social creatures and really do need and enjoy fellowship with each other. Make sure that he doesn't get much of that at church and perhaps you can convince him that he is more likely to fulfill the need at whatever social club you can get him to join. More than likely, this will really mean at their bar, where "everybody knows his name".

With Worst Regards,
Wormwood

CHAPTER 9

From: Wormwood <wormwood@gehenna.email>

Sent: Saturday, June 8, 2019 2:30 AM

To: Wart Hog <warthog@gehenna.email>

Subject: Eternal Security and Cheap Grace

My Dear Wart Hog,

I can see that we will have to review some of the basics. You really are a bit stale, aren't you? Despite my last email, you still seem overly afraid that your man has "become a Christian". Remember, to be a true believer consists of far more than just walking to the front at the end of a church service or even in parroting back a little prayer talk. Knowledge of God is often very far removed from the love of Him.

I assure you that many of those who claim to be Christians and perhaps even completely believe it themselves are not in fact, Christians at all. It will be more than a little amusing to see the look of shock on their faces when they are met and claimed by Our Father Below!

Of course, you and I cannot know for sure which of the humans has truly crossed the line into the Enemy's camp. Similarly, in the case of those who have made such a move, we don't know for certain whether our efforts can or cannot bring them back over to our side again. We merely know that whatever the costs, we must continue the fight.

R.J. Aldridge

As to their real condition, all we know is that some humans are easier for us to work on and others are not. That noxious cloud, which has been viciously rumored to be the Spirit of the Enemy himself, appears thicker and stronger around certain humans and less so around others. Alas, you may find out that when it is at its thickest, it is nearly impossible for us to make meaningful progress with them at all.

It is only when they pass on from their temporary mortal state into the eternal one when we will know which side of the conflict has won that particular human soul. That is when they are claimed for all eternity by Our Father Below or the Enemy with no chances at reincarnations or other second chances.

As you know, the humans have proven over thousands of years that they cannot live by the law of righteousness that the nature of God requires. Nothing new there, for if the standard is true perfection, not many will prove worthy by their own efforts to enter into the presence of such a holy God. What the Enemy did to fix this problem and to provide a means for their salvation was the shocker. He took the entire burden upon Himself!

This was done by the unique creation of a perfect union of God and man, in the form of Jesus the Christ. As God, He could live a perfect life under the law and in an act of sacrificial substitution, provided a type of replacement for the humans who could never do so on their own. Horribly unfair to us, I admit, to bring in such a "ringer" as Himself. The little vermin should have to try to fulfill all the laws on their own, then we would surely get every last one of them.

Well, regardless of my wishful thinking on the subject, Jesus has offered to each and every one of the humans his sacrificial death as a substitute for their own. All they have to do is admit, before God and themselves, that they are sinful and in need of the salvation that is offered to them and are willing to take Jesus as Lord and Savior. In my opinion, this is where our opportunity arises. You will find that many of the humans are happy to take Jesus as

The Wormwood Emails

Savior but to take him as Lord is quite another thing!

If you ever get to hear one of the human preachers rant and rave about hellfire and brimstone, you will understand what I mean. To hear them go on, you could almost begin to think that hell is quite an intolerable place after all. During such a message, only a complete idiot wouldn't take Jesus as Savior in order to escape such a fate. He is, after all, offered to them completely free of charge; "without cost or obligation", you might say. In light of all that, why not walk the aisle? Why not say a little prayer, perhaps even silently? Where is the cost or harm in that? Is salvation not proffered as a type of free of charge, eternal, infernal fire insurance policy?

I have known humans who do all of the above and spend most of their lives pretending to be true believers but never really fully believe at all. I think that if we could ask them why they continue in such a charade, that their answers could ultimately be boiled down to something along the lines of "just in case". They seem to think that a halfhearted belief in a Christ who might be only imaginary after all is faith enough to save them.

To take Jesus as Lord, however, is something quite different. To look to Him as Lord, they must believe completely in Him and in His strength to deliver. A Lord is someone who is respected, admired and even feared a bit at times. Above all else, a Lord is to be obeyed, and in a very real sense, one who "owns" another as a master might own his serf or slave.

The advocates of the doctrine of cheap grace should know better. I wonder like James, the brother or Jesus did, how walking down the aisle can eternally save a man, if he has no change of heart or resulting change of lifestyle? To the early Christians, the word "repent", as in "repent and be saved" doesn't mean just to feel sorry about something. To regret one's past life and want to escape the fires of hell is only a part of the picture. In the Biblical sense, to repent actually meant to change one's mind or purpose in living. It is as if you physically turn around, from living your life your own

R.J. Aldridge

way to attempt to live it for the Enemy and in doing so, to try to be like Jesus. Imitation remains the sincerest form of admiration.

So where is the opportunity for us? It is simply in the fact that many who consider themselves Christians, read the Bible, sit in the churches (or even preach in them) may not be in the Enemy's Camp at all. Perhaps they had an emotional experience at one point in time, perhaps they "made a decision" for God, but what of that? If they haven't acknowledged Jesus as Lord, as the early disciples and apostles did, they may not be His after all.

You would think that some would suspect this, particularly in light of what Jesus said in the Gospels about the "many" who will call him Lord and perform miracles in His name and yet will not enter into heaven. He even says that these will have cast out demons and done marvelous works in his name. Does He not call them "workers of iniquity"? Why? Because they were doing it all for themselves and for their own glorification and not for His. They may have called him Savior but He never really was their Lord.

So even if you see your man going to church, singing the hymns and saying "Amen" from time to time, don't despair too much. If we could look into his heart, like the Enemy can, we could see what his condition really is. In the meantime, we just have to do our best and assume that he isn't really a believer after all. In any case, we must act on them until the final hour and indeed, the final second of their lives. To paraphrase a human saying, the game isn't over until the fat lady dies.

With Worst Regards,
Wormwood

CHAPTER 10

From: Wormwood <wormwood@gehenna.email>

Sent: Tuesday, August 13, 2019 5:55 AM

To: Wart Hog <warthog@gehenna.email>

Subject: An Ideal Mate

My Dear Wart Hog,

Yes, you may be right about trying to marry off your patient. If nothing else, it could be an excellent diversionary tactic. We certainly don't want him to dedicate himself to serving the Enemy and his Church. That reprehensible man, Saul of Tarsus, was correct when he said that a single man could focus on pleasing God, but that a married man must also try to please his wife. So, why don't you hurry up and find him a suitable mate?

You will remember that the male of their species is attracted primarily to physical beauty. His head may believe that such beauty is only skin deep, but fortunately for us his glands march to a different drummer. Your first efforts should be along this path.

Try to partner him up with an attractive but shallow and self-centered female. It is often true that these women are what the Americans have sometimes called "air heads". Perhaps I should refer to them as "BAH" (beautiful air headed) women? Yes, I rather like that acronym. While their less attractive sisters were doing their lessons in school, the BAHs were more concerned about

51

learning how to apply makeup for greatest effect.

As a BAH generally judges the value of everything by its relative attractiveness, they are unusually more concerned about their wardrobe, the house they live in, their furniture, the car they drive, etc. When your self-worth comes from being better looking than those around you, it is hard not to make a similar value judgment with regards to everything else that you own.

Needless to say, to always have the most attractive, the newest and the latest is also significantly more expensive. I believe you reported that your man is solidly in the middle classes as to matters of income and assets. Well then, a woman of this type will be a constant financial burden to him. No matter how much money he can earn, she will always spend even more!

Over the years, he will likely become a hopeless workaholic, spending more and more time at the office in an effort to satisfy her insatiable material desires. Truth to tell, he will also be trying to escape her company as well, for you see, a man needs the respect of his wife more than anything else in a relationship. Even if she doesn't openly complain about how much he earns, which a BAH often will, he will feel less and less adequate to her and therefore, in his own eyes as well. If the marriage lasts at all, it will be distant and above all else, focused primarily on material acquisitions.

Yes, I would recommend the Beautiful Air Head as a primary target. They are fairly common today, you know, and more than the normal distribution has gravitated to the Los Angeles area. Something about the entertainment industry there, I believe. I know that he is likely to get bored to tears shortly after the honeymoon, as he finds his new wife woefully inadequate other than as a type of ornamental decoration but by then, he'll be quite stuck with her.

If you cannot locate a suitable BAH, then I would suggest looking for a "disappointed angry feminist", or shall we call her a DAF? There are quite a few of these around these days as well, although

The Wormwood Emails

the numbers have dropped a bit over the last few decades. The DAF is convinced that the world has been particularly unfair to women, that men have been the primary instigator behind these inequities and that other than the reproductive glands, men and women are essentially alike.

Some of the inequities that they see are real, of course, and very often women haven't been adequately valued within many of earth's societies. A true DAF has taken this truth and blown it out of all proportion. As an example, they will point to income disparities between the sexes and fail to adjust for the differences in the occupations being compared, educational levels achieved, the years on the job or other relevant variables. It is, so to speak, an "apples to oranges" comparison.

The truth is that the Enemy has chosen to make women and men different in very many ways, right down to the cellular level. I'm not sure as to the why of it, as we demons obviously aren't burdened with the curse of gender. I would surmise that the roles of male and female have something to do with the different facets of God's own nature. After all, He stated that He created the humans in His own image, "male and female He created them".

We have long puzzled on the apparent differences in the Enemy's approach to humankind, seeming rather refreshingly harsh with them in the Old Testament and so disgustingly loving and merciful in the New Testament. Perhaps, like the human male, part of his character is focused on protecting, providing, leading and when necessary, disciplining as well. Yet like the female, could another facet to His nature be primarily focused on forgiveness, demonstrative love, loyalty and service?

In any case the DAF female will be one who is diligently trying to ignore the differences but may condescend to marry in recognition of the biological necessity of having a man involved in reproduction. Two things are likely to happen in such a relationship and both will help our cause. First, she will be hypersensitive to everything he does, for as a member of the oppressive (meaning

53

R.J. Aldridge

the male) class, she will unconsciously expect him to try to take advantage of her at every opportunity. Secondly, she will insist on what she calls "equality", but really means that she wants to deny the intrinsic differences that their respective genders demand.

In the first case, you will note lots of motivations are misconstrued and active fighting results. The second case is more insidious, for it results in a passive discontent and frustration. It is amusing, for you will see that if her man is willing and able to play the role of the "sensitive male", by which she means someone like her on the inside and appearing to be male on the outside, she will seldom be satisfied with the hybrid that they have created. Like it or not, she is one half of a pair that together form a complete whole. The Enemy said that the "two shall be one" and we must assume that as the Designer, He knew what He was talking about.

I trust that after the Franklin Graham incident, I don't have to remind you that the woman must not, under any circumstances, be a Christian? If you can get one that is nonreligious or dedicated to any of the nice alternative religions we wrote about earlier, so much the better. I think that you will find a man who will go to any church when his wife is indifferent to them is a rarity. Usually, it is the female who influences the male to attend, very seldom the other way around.

With Worst Regards,
Wormwood

CHAPTER 11

From: Wormwood <wormwood@gehenna.email>

Sent: Tuesday, August 27, 2019 2:55 AM

To: Wart Hog <warthog@gehenna.email>

Subject: Human Occupations

My Dear Wart Hog,

Frankly, it matters very little to either the Enemy or to us, as to what your man chooses for his occupation. Unless you can induce him into something that is not only sinful for him and harmful to society as well; such as being a drug dealer, thief or pornographer, it is of little concern to us and seldom has any intrinsic benefit in securing his damnation. Always remember, we care only about his eternal soul, not how he spends his days earning a living during his short stay on earth.

Your man may think that the Enemy might prefer it if he were a missionary or minister, but I'm not sure that this is often the case. As far as I can tell, He made them with differing abilities and likings and seems more concerned that they do their work well, whatever that work may be. The Apostle Paul said that "Whatsoever you do, do it as unto the Lord". I firmly believe that the Enemy would rather see a good and honest Christian plumber doing excellent work, helping his fellows and testifying of the Christ than to see the same man struggling to be a mediocre minister. If he is ill suited for that role, his sincerity does not necessar-

55

R.J. Aldridge

ily overcome his incompetence.

Nevertheless, I grant that it is an important issue to your man at least, so it would be best if we discuss it further. The first thing that you should realize, if you don't already, is that most men derive much of their sense of "who they are" based upon their occupation. More than that, it is often their measure of status and achievement in their world. Observe your patient and his interactions with other men. When they meet for the first time, almost invariably one of the first questions asked is along the lines of "What do you do for a living?". One method of attacking him, therefore, is through his work. Make him unhappy and unfulfilled in it and there can be much that you will accomplish elsewhere.

You may, by the way, find the modern world of work a bit strange when compared with your prior assignments during the middle ages. In those days, most of the labor that people did was done in concert with their families and often in or near their own homes. From farmer to tradesman, the men worked next to their fathers, uncles and grandfathers. Often, their own sons would eventually take up the trade after the older generation's time had passed. In a similar manner, the women passed on home making and other skills to their daughters. With few exceptions, it was generally a family or community effort all round.

Things have changed a lot recently due to what they called the industrial revolution. In the urge to centralize, due to "economies of scale" and other axioms of the economists, there was a marked shift to larger scale manufacturing. This rapidly led to a massive shift out of the home, farm and small shop and into the large factory or office.

This may sound like a small thing to you, but the fabric of society and of the family itself changed considerably. To many, Dad became a man who left early in the morning and returned, too exhausted to do much more than to eat and sleep, late in the evening. His role was simplified to a source of money and an occasional dispenser of painful discipline. Sort of a cross between a

The Wormwood Emails

banker and a policeman, so to speak, and just about as popular.

The schools followed suit and took over the education of the young, usually in large institutionalized settings. As a result, the parents no longer are the primary teachers of their own children. Further, the children are out of the homes for most of the productive portion of the day. Like Dad, they sometimes seem more like visitors than residents. Economic pressures of the last fifty years have added Mom to the equation as she is also off to the workplace, leaving the younger ones in the care of others and the older ones to fend for themselves after school.

One funny thing about humans is that where they spend most of their time usually becomes the most important part of their lives. If you spend 40 plus hours at work, for example, it is only natural that it becomes something of great concern to you. Today, Mom and Dad are generally more concerned about what their boss thinks of them than their spouse's opinion. The children, in turn, are more worried about being popular with the other students than with Mom and Dad. As to their willingness to believe that any information they hear is true, just ask any ten-year-old if they believe their parents or the teacher to be right on any question remotely related to academics. They will go with the teacher every time.

You see the point? We not only have far more to time to work on them individually, without the bothersome concerns of a family about them, but often can also make real progress at restructuring their value systems to accommodate our own agendas.

Like the Enemy, we are primarily concerned about the motivations and attitudes behind his actions. We can often get a man to quite literally "lie, cheat and steal" to get ahead at his work, in pursuit of a promotion, greater influence and income. There is nothing wrong with ambition, of course, or even in trying to "get ahead". This desire is merely a manifestation of certain virtues given by the Enemy, such as willingness to work hard, creativity and perseverance. If the man is ambitious because he wishes to

R.J. Aldridge

serve God, his family and mankind better, then this is harmful to our cause and pleasing to the Enemy. What we require is ambition that is fully focused upon self, rather than upon others. Luckily for us, the human soul has a naturally bent in that direction already. It takes a lot of work by the Enemy to make a man live his life otherwise.

With Worst Regards,
Wormwood

CHAPTER 12

From: Wormwood <wormwood@gehenna.email>

Sent: Thursday, May 14, 2020 12:49 AM

To: Wart Hog <warthog@gehenna.email>

Subject: Mature Christians?

My Dear Wart Hog,

Let's review, shall we? Your man still believes himself to be a Christian, but you have been able to make him a very active church shopper, seldom being with the same congregation more than a week or two before looking for something better (or at least something different). Keep it up and I think you will find that he loses much of his earlier enthusiasm for Christianity, as he will receive little spiritual nourishment from the church and little or no fellowship with other Christians. With any luck, you can reclaim him from his temporary foray into the Enemy's domain and let him come to feel a bit of smug satisfaction about the "religious phase" which he has felt himself to outgrow.

As we discussed before, keep him focused on the outward nature of religion, the church buildings, etc. for this will allow him to think himself "spiritual", without ever giving serious consideration to the true state of his own soul. I would guess that at this stage, his faith, if faith it really is, is largely cosmetic anyway. He is trying to look and sound like the other Christians that he encounters at church, or at least the ones that he feels are worthy of

59

R.J. Aldridge

such emulation. In his heart, however he knows that his faith is quite shallow and superficial. In short, he is still play acting.

He can often be led to believe for a very long time that his faith will deepen only when he is "properly instructed" from the pulpit. This places the burden for his own spiritual growth on the minister and not upon himself. If the minister is "boring"; well, he himself can't really be blamed, can he? In fact, it is very probable that he will strengthen his faith only to the extent that he makes a personal effort to do so. The recommended path is a simple one and includes such things as reading the Bible regularly, earnest and frequent prayer, avoidance of sin, service to others, witnessing, etc. In this complicated world of theirs, we have convinced many that these simple truths are "too simple" and therefore, must not be the truth at all.

You may wish to encourage him to continue to view himself as a spiritual newcomer and as such, not the one who should carry the message of Christianity to the unbelieving. The fact that he is indeed a newcomer to each church that he visits may help in this attempt. If he can be held back from any real service to others based upon his immaturity in the faith, while at the same time having him neglect those very things which might serve to bring him to such maturity, you have carried off a very fine balancing act. Before he knows it, he will be physically too old to be able to do anything at all, even while he remains a spiritual infant.

The perception that only mature Christians can have any impact on the world is false, of course, but what is true will almost always be subordinated to what he believes. You may remember that the early Christian church which made great advances for the Enemy consisted largely of people who had very little to assist them in that effort, other that the Spirit of the Enemy himself. Often it is the new converts, fresh and excited about it all, that do the most damage to our cause. Give me an older complacent Christian any day!

In the days of the early church, they didn't even have the scrip-

The Wormwood Emails

tures in anything but small fragments, and no one had a personal copy. Today, the Bible is probably one of the easiest things to obtain. If the *New York Times* bestseller list were compiled correctly, then the Bible would perennially be in the top ten. Luckily, its very commonness has worked against it, so that although the Bible may be a major best seller, once purchased and taken home, it usually becomes only a dust collector.

Just as he thinks that spiritual changes will occur within him due to the influences of the minister, humans are always looking for ways to improve themselves which come from the "outside inwards". As an aside, this can be a great weapon against them. They seem to think that virtually all changes, for the good or for the ill, begin with the externalities.

They go to college to become more intelligent, as if knowledge were assimilated through osmosis and not by study. They join a health club to get in shape, as if occasionally hanging around the gymnasium in sports attire will accomplish what only regular exercise and perspiration will bring about. Perhaps that is why they place such an emphasis on the beauty that really proves skin deep after all, trying to preserve throughout their lifetimes what veneer of surface attractiveness the Enemy has allotted to them.

We know as God does, that real and lasting changes always proceed from the inside outwards. Your man will be looking for a minister to change him by virtue of things that he hears, or thinks he hears, spoken from the pulpit. For change to be permanent, it must effect his most inward being. Merely intellectually assenting to the truth of God (or any other truth) won't change the man or hurt our cause. It is only when the truth comes into his "heart" and is incorporated into his value system, goals, desires and habits that it does us any real harm. Like the Enemy's story about the seed, the heart must be receptive for the seed to be fruitful. Remember, "...none so deaf as those who will not hear".

I take it that he is generally discontent with his work, partly due to the work itself and partly due to the fact that he doesn't perceive it as being very "Christian". This brings to mind another, very important point about the humans. They naturally look at their lives as divided into different areas; such as work, finance, family, social, sexual, intellectual, athletics, etc. Try to get him to continue to live his life in just such a segmented and compartmentalized fashion. It is important to have him look at his spiritual life as just another piece of the pie, so to speak, and that his Christianity can be treated merely as a small portion of the whole.

If you can fully exploit this tendency, he can be encouraged to be a largely different man in each of the lives that he inhabits. At work, he can be encouraged to be ruthless and dishonest, because after all, "business is business". In his financial affairs, he will resent the relatively modest offerings given to the churches he visits as he is having a difficult enough time making ends meet anyway. He may feel a bit guilty about his extramarital sex life, but it is, after all, "only natural".

Do you see where I'm going with this? If necessary, we will begrudgingly grant him the hour or two on Sunday morning if we can retain control on everything else. This can even add a bit of fun to the sometimes tedious life of the tempter, as you will be able to work on making him a great hypocrite as he attempts to be Christian on Sunday and anything else but from Monday morning until Saturday night.

What you don't want him ever to realize is that the Christian life is not designed to be another piece in his "pie of life". What the Christian life is designed to be (and to be lived successfully it must be) the entire pie itself. His work life must be undertaken with his Christian beliefs throughout, as must be the case in every other area of his living. All his actions, decisions and ideals should reflect his Christian beliefs and to do less is simply to be less than a complete Christian. The Enemy desires that His Spirit permeate and more often than not, to change every element of the man's existence. We must continue to work for the divisions.

The Wormwood Emails

So by all means keep him church shopping and if possible, shopping for women as well. With his glands in their current state of hyper production, you should be able to steer him fairly easily towards the attractive, but vacuous and self-centered ones. Perhaps someone at his place of work? Perhaps someone already married? This might allow us to break up a family as well as provide him with a mate who will likely be very satisfactory to our purposes. Someone who is unfaithful to their current spouse in order to be with him is just as likely to repeat the offense to be with someone else later on.

With Worst Regards,
Wormwood

CHAPTER 13

From: Wormwood <wormwood@gehenna.email>

Sent: Monday, May 25, 2020 2:18 AM

To: Wart Hog <warthog@gehenna.email>

Subject: Astrology and Psychics

My Dear Wart Hog,

Why didn't you tell me earlier that your man is interested in astrology? Did you think this such a little thing, as he is also still a practicing Christian? It may, in fact, be a small thing now, but you still have a toehold of paganism in him. Don't underestimate what opportunities this affords us.

You may be unaware of the fact that certain departments of Low Command have been working at adding layer upon layer of superstitions and pagan like beliefs into modern North America and much of Europe as well. For once, I am glad to report that they have exceeded all expectations for success. Please note that the primary emphasis has been to add pagan practices, not to substitute them for mainstream religious beliefs. The idea is not to convince people that Christianity is wrong, per se, but simply to add so many other superstitions as to completely cloud the basic Christian message.

Astrology, of course, is an old one that we have used for thousands of years. You would be surprised how many humans think that the stars that visibly present in the sky at the time of their birth can somehow have an affect on their personalities and destinies in life.

From astrology, it is only a short step to the other techniques for "knowing" the future and making up one's mind about current courses of action. They pay fortune tellers, now largely referred to as "psychics", to tell them what to do and what the future holds. Why they don't find it odd that these psychics charge them only a relatively modest sum on an hourly basis for such information is astonishing. If those doing the advising really knew what the future held, would they not just buy the correct stocks on the New York Stock Exchange, or chose the right numbers for the next lottery, or spend time at the local horserace track? Why sell your knowledge of the future for $30 per session, if you can simply take it along to Las Vegas?

The psychics cannot see the future, of course, and what little they seem to know about the present we whisper in their ears. Jesus told his followers to "take no worry about tomorrow" and to trust in the Enemy to supply their needs. In fact, the Bible clearly and specifically speaks against fortune telling. Luckily, both their curiosity and their fears help us negate this advice.

Look around the church the next time your man attends. You will see people wearing some of the same type of amulets that you may remember as being worn in medieval times for good luck or protection. Others will have pieces of crystal hung around their necks, looking to enhance their abilities or to increase personal power. Some avoid black cats, walking under a ladder or anything to do with the number thirteen.

Their search for personal fulfillment often runs broad enough to include almost anything offered to them. Like a shallow flood, their belief systems may run through the church but can encompass everything else in the area as well. Luckily for us, their convictions are broad but not deep. Based on how most of them pursue knowing the Enemy, about at the ankles, I should think.

By doing this, they fall prey to so many of our devices. For-

R.J. Aldridge

tune tellers of various types, readers of auras and palms, wearing charms and crystals, chanting and channeling, fire walking or other tricks of the fakirs, the list is quite long nowadays. If you can bury his Christianity under enough of these, you can largely suffocate it.

Rather than studying the scriptures to learn how they should live, they study the stars and their charts instead. Instead of trusting in God to provide for their "daily bread" and their future needs, they try to find out what that future may hold through any number of extraordinary means and employ certain rituals to help it along. Instead of praying for change within themselves, enlisting the power of the Spirit to help to bring it about, they think that what they wear about their necks may do the trick.

I know what you are thinking and no, most of them don't seem to grasp the inconsistencies inherent in trying to take both positions. Many practitioners of these and other superstitions beliefs still believe themselves to be Christian. If they are, it is a strange Christianity indeed, that simultaneously puts faith in such things alongside and on equal footing as to their faith in God.

Personally, I think that it all goes back to their basic tendency, fostered by us for these many years, not to look at ideas in terms as basic as whether they are "right or wrong". If a new concept is interesting to them, or if it may be useful towards the accomplishment of a goal that they have set up for themselves, then what is the harm of taking it on? That it may indirectly or even directly contradict the teachings of the Enemy and of his Christ seems not to be considered by many of them.

If you asked a thousand of the human adults living in America to describe the spiritual state of their nation, I think they would say that there is a growing climate of what they might call "rationality" or "secular humanism" over traditional religion. In truth, the USA is largely neo-pagan and steeped in idolatry, much to our delight.

The same man who expounds on Darwin and the wonders

wrought by evolution is likely to see Gaia, the ancient earth goddess, lurking in the fields and the forests. The woman who scoffs at the Bible's miracles believes in reincarnation and that she was a maid to Cleopatra in a prior lifetime. The man who doubts the power of prayer to change things will make sure that he wears his "lucky tie" and carries a rabbit's foot to work when he is trying to land that big account. The woman who doubts whether a true prophet from God can know the future will pay a clairvoyant at the local county fair to advise her instead.

The Enemy calls them sheep, which as you know is an animal which is very easily deceived. Sometimes it is far easier to bury the Enemy's truth than to try to defeat it. Easier still to confuse the humans into burying it themselves.

With Worst Regards,

Wormwood

CHAPTER 14

From: Wormwood <wormwood@gehenna.email>

Sent: Monday, July 20, 2020 1:26 AM

To: Wart Hog <warthog@gehenna.email>

Subject: A Local Church

My Dear Wart Hog,

I am sorry to hear that your man has joined a church. How did that sneak up on you? You said that he went to one of those after service "coffee fellowships" and found one of the young women serving to be quite to his liking, but to join a church to try to meet her seems a bit extreme. Couldn't you have convinced him that there are other pretty women yet to be discovered at other churches and kept him on his rounds? That an even more attractive woman might appear some day?

Perhaps I'm just peeved because one of our lures, physical attraction, has seemed to work against us this time. I'd be making no protests if the church he had joined was a spiritually dead one, but in this case, the fool did the wrong thing for the right reason. Yes, unfortunately, my research shows that it is a thriving establishment, where the Bible is not only taught but actually believed and that the worship of God is both enthusiastic and sincere. All in all, a very unhealthy place from which you had better extricate him as soon as possible!

If you can't get him to leave quickly, however, don't despair too

The Wormwood Emails

much, for I have heard from some of the tempters assigned to others in this church and there is hope yet. In fact, the very best of hopes where such a church is concerned. What I mean, of course, is the possibility that a "church split" is brewing. Nothing that I know so retards the growth of a church body than to have it ripped apart, not unlike what happens in a formerly strong marriage that ends in a bitter and lengthy divorce.

The oldest of friends can become cold and distant overnight. Those who leave will likely resent the time and money that they invested in the activities of the church they left behind. Those who stay will likely suffer through feelings of both doubt and pride, both very useful emotions for us. Some will be unsure about that decision and will experience concerns as to whether they made the right choice. This may turn them again into critics, as they look for the negatives that they apparently missed before. Those who stay and are sure that the choice was the correct one, can often fall into pride that they are the "true believers" and unspoken, but very real, resentment towards those "apostates" who left their fold.

In any case, the church body that remains will often experience significant money problems, as they attempt to maintain the same facilities, staff and programs with fewer congregants. Often, we can tempt them to reduce giving to the poor, to missionaries and other outreach programs as unnecessary when compared to paying the mortgage or not laying off any of the ministerial staff.

Those who leave may simply join another congregation, but I find it much better for us if we encourage them to start yet another church with the resulting needs to hire a Pastor, locate a building to rent (or build), etc. They will find it much more expensive than they think, replacing everything from hymn books to baby cribs. Even more than those they left behind at the old church, they will be tempted to spend all the offerings on themselves. It warms my heart to think of how many additional souls we may capture while this new church acquires a building, adds a multi-purpose

R.J. Aldridge

room and then buys a church bus; all the while spending money that might have been more wisely spent trying to reach souls for the cause of Christ before it is too late.

If a split happens and your man begins to feel any concern about this obvious misplacement of priorities, plant in his mind the need to "build a strong base" before undertaking outreach activities. Often, they will build their base for years! Besides, the chances are good that before the base is built to their complete satisfaction, the new church can be split to start this process all over again, ad infinitum.

This inherent divisiveness, or "denominationalism", has plagued the church from the very beginning. As early as Corinth, there were groups that followed Paul, Peter, Apollos, etc. How fortunate for us that the modern church is also ridden with such a tendency towards disunity! It almost makes a complete mockery of their claims to be of "...one Lord, one faith and one baptism..." to realize that there are now hundreds if not thousands of distinct "Christian" denominations or subgroups represented just in America alone.

Of course, on a national and international scale, the job of encouraging the creation of divisions and factions within the church is a task for demons far more advanced than ourselves within the Low Command. We can only offer them our congratulations on a job well done, while enjoying the opportunities that this affords within our individual human patients.

You may ask how to encourage church splits? The answer is surprisingly easy, as all humans are prone to mistakes. If you can just get them to focus on those of others and to forget about their own, then you are setting them up for disappointments and eventually for anger as well. Keep their minds off Christ's parable about the "mote and beam" or forgiveness "seventy times seven". Don't let them realize that they are exhibiting the same attitude that Christ condemned in the Pharisees of His time, who expected more holiness of others than they were willing or able to perform themselves.

A first-rate church split can get your man generally down on others and perhaps on Christianity itself, as he is a new convert to the faith. He may still be acting under the subconscious expectation that Christians are "better than" everyday humans. In many cases, I have heard of Christians who literally turned from their faith. Don't let him suspect that his standard of perfection in others is both unrealistic and unfair. Don't let him consider that those who have disappointed him within the church may not be Christians at all, or perhaps too new to know any better. Whatever you do, don't let him suspect that flaws in the way people present God's message does not, by any means, invalidate the message itself.

With Worst Regards,
Wormwood

CHAPTER 15

From: Wormwood <wormwood@gehenna.email>

Sent: Friday, October 16, 2020 2:52 AM

To: Wart Hog <warthog@gehenna.email>

Subject: Sin and Forgiveness

My Dear Wart Hog,

While you are waiting around for the church he is attending to self-destruct, let's see what we can do to frustrate any further efforts on his part towards spiritual maturity. Perhaps you can shake the foundations of his faith a little bit.

Have you tried questioning the completeness of God's forgiveness? This is particularly effective for many humans, you know, as they often have a difficult time forgiving other people of their offenses. Truth to tell, they even find it difficult to forgive themselves sometimes.

The fact that he has sinned is obvious, even to him, who probably notes and remembers only a small, token few of the vast number of offenses that he has committed. For that matter, humans remember next to nothing of their failures to do what they should have done and did not, nor of the offenses which they only thought about. All of these can be sins nonetheless.

When he made the decision to accept Christ as Savior, part of the arrangement was that he would receive forgiveness from God for

The Wormwood Emails

all of his sins. If your man is one who holds a grudge against others who have wronged or offended him, try sneaking the thought in that the Enemy, if even half as holy and just as they claim that He is, must have an even more difficult time with true forgiveness. If you can get him to worry about whether his offenses will be cast back in his face someday, his fears of being ultimately rejected in the end will nag at him constantly. No one likes the thought of being turned away from the Pearly Gates, do they?

A man in this state will ask for forgiveness repetitively and the more often he asks, the less confidence he will have as to having received absolution. I don't know how the Enemy feels about having to hear the same requests over and over again, when He has already promised to forgive as well as forget, but I know that I would get rather annoyed.

Even if you cannot pull off the nagging fear diversion, by all means try to lay a thick layer of guilt on him. He may be convinced that God has forgiven him, but that He really shouldn't have, as the man cannot fully forgive himself. Guilt can be even more immobilizing to him than fear, as the former is fixed upon events that cannot be changed. Feeling guilty over sins that God has forgiven is really a form of pride, isn't it? What he is really saying is that the forgiveness which is good enough for the Enemy isn't quite good enough for him.

We've touched before upon the great complaint laid against the church, that it is filled with hypocrites. I think that this has been one of our greatest triumphs in undermining the church as a whole and people's willingness to attend. Of course, the church is filled by hypocrites! It is filled with humans and all of them to some degree and at some time have acted in a hypocritical manner. For what is a hypocrite, save one who advocates and pretends one way of living while living less than that standard?

Praise to Our Father Below, they all still have sinful natures, so they all live something less than the perfect lives that the Enemy demands and that they espouse. Honestly, not going to church because it is "filled with hypocrites" is something like saying that you won't go to the hospital because it is "filled with sick people". Filled with hypocrites it may be, but as they are wont to say, "there is always room for one more".

Where we have difficulties is within churches that openly recognize this fact. They pursue holiness, to be sure, but help each other along the way when one of them stumbles. If you can get them all to pretend perfection and to openly declare that everything is wonderful whenever they may be asked, you will be at a great advantage. Generally, it is only when such deceit is added that hypocrisy really armor plates them against the Enemy. Was not one of the Christ's complaints against the religious leaders of His day that they refused to admit that they were sinful and therefore in need of salvation? This is the type of hypocrite that we delight in.

The last topic is a particularly painful one, but I must voice it nonetheless. I think you may have guessed what I am leading up to so steel yourself... worship. When I hear the word, I get an inkling of what the humans must feel when they walk past a dentist's office and hear the high-pitched whine of the drill. Even though the doctor isn't working on their own teeth, the pangs of discomfort come sympathetically.

I don't know to what extent you have had to endure it, but my man attends a church every Sunday morning that really knows how to worship. In a fit of self-forgetfulness, they praise the Enemy and all that He is with heartfelt enthusiasm. Naturally, I loathe every minute of it!

To escape the clouds of the Enemy's righteousness and peace that come down upon the place, not to mention getting away from my own resulting personal pain, I generally have to flee to a little tavern a couple of counties over. Often it's Monday afternoon or Tuesday morning before I can get back on track again.

I pity you if your man goes to such a place. If he does not, keep him away from any kind of true praise and worship at all costs.

The Wormwood Emails

Perhaps he is fool enough to think that just coldly mouthing a few words will be enough. Many of them do, you know, even complaining if hymns are used that are less than two hundred years old. Not aged enough to qualify them as "holy", I suppose.

With Worst Regards,
Wormwood

CHAPTER 16

From: Wormwood <wormwood@gehenna.email>

Sent: Saturday, October 24, 2020 1:59 AM

To: Wart Hog <warthog@gehenna.email>

Subject: Pain and Suffering

My Dear Wart Hog,

It was interesting to meet you at the GNAT convention last weekend. I usually have a horrible time at the Greater North American Tempters meetings so of course, I look forward to them immensely. May I offer you a compliment in saying that you are even more hideous in the flesh, so to speak, than what your correspondence might indicate?

Hopefully your man didn't make any marked improvements in his relationship to the Enemy while you were gone. Mine is so complacent in his "faith", he doesn't even seem to realize that he could, in fact, advance much further in the Enemy's camp if he would only make the smallest efforts to do so.

I was reflecting on our conversations about pain and suffering and can see how you are far the greater expert in this area. It would appear that I have somehow fallen into the common trap of assuming that anything that is unpleasant to them is therefore good for us. While this is often true when it comes to their physical pain and mental sufferings, I can see that it may not always be the case. It is hard to believe that I failed to see the correlation with

The Wormwood Emails

the First Rule for Tempters, that anything which can move the patient closer to the Enemy is to be used sparingly, if at all. I hope that you won't mention this oversight on my part to our superiors at Low Command.

I would suppose that some of my error comes from the fact that the humans seem to hate pain so very much and undertake every possible means to avoid it. Particularly in the western world, pain is often looked upon as something that is always a

negative. So much of their time and effort seems to be directed to the avoidance of any kind of physical discomfort at any time. Naturally, it makes one want to use it to make their lives miserable whenever possible.

After all, everywhere they go, from the house to the office, in the car to the market, from the church to the restaurant, they try to maintain the maximum level of physical comfort possible. When they are going to someplace that might prove unpleasant, like the dentist's office, they take every precaution possible to avoid pain through the use of topical and local anesthetics, inhalation of calming gas, music to distract them playing in their ears, etc. If a headache or other bodily pain does somehow manage to sneak its way into their lives, it's off to the medicine cabinet for a pain killer at once and then to the doctor for something stronger if that doesn't do the trick.

As to suffering, which I will define here to be the discomfort of the mind that arises from events in their lives which they look upon as "unfortunate", they also seek avoidance. This is done by virtue of attempts to provide security for themselves and for their possessions. They avoid risks when they can and buy insurance to cover the risks which cannot be avoided.

To protect where they live; insurance on their homes, furniture, clothes and other belongings. On their vehicles; car, boat or other similar coverage. For their bodies; life, disability, medical and dental insurance. For their money; deposit insurance at the bank, securities coverage for their stocks and bonds and personal liabil-

R.J. Aldridge

ity insurance to protect against lawsuits. For those in business, duplication of all of these protections for their stock and trade. Finally, to protect the soundness of the protectors themselves, they make sure that the insurance companies are insured against default.

Being so swathed in such layers of "protection", they are still disappointed and often angry when misfortune does come their way. They may have insurance, but they still hate the thought of wrecking the car or having a fire at their home. Even if the insurance company bears most of the financial costs involved, such an event is still an inconvenience to them and they really do despise inconveniences.

As to medicine and the impact on the human body, someone else may be paying the hospital bills, but they themselves must endure the suffering. Suffer they do, Wart Hog, not just in their minds as they worry about what the illness means to them and to others, but often in the body as well when the realities of physical pain makes its presence known. I assure you, they would give over this activity to another as well, if an insurance policy could be devised that could undertake such a transfer.

Of course, there are many things which can befall them for which they cannot fully prepare. If they are farmers, the rains may not be enough for the crops, or the weather can be too cold or too hot. If they are fishermen, the catch may be poor and the conditions arduous. Any businessman can find that a change in government rules and regulations may hurt sales or can even put him out of business. Even the average worker, who may think himself immune from such shocks, can find that they lose their jobs entirely.

Most of the humans seem to consider physical pain and mental sufferings are the primary evils in life, sometimes being viewed as even worse than death itself. They are far more concerned about remaining temporarily comfortable in the bodily state than to be eternally blissful when their short lives on earth are completed. In this lies a tremendous opportunity.

The Wormwood Emails

If they don't already believe in God, things are easier for us. When pain and suffering come along, as they inevitably will in time, we get them to assume this as further evidence that God must not exist at all. In any case, not the Christian God who is declared to be both "loving" and "all powerful". They reason that if there were such a God, He would never permit such suffering to occur if He had the power to stop it. Since pain and suffering irrefutably exist, then the Christian God must not.

For those who already have some degree of faith in God, the case is a bit harder for us but by no means hopeless. We are aided in this by well-intentioned ministers who preach, perhaps with too much zeal and far too often, about a Jesus who will meet every need and answer every problem. This is sometimes misunderstood by the listeners to mean that He will prevent anything from entering their lives that will cause a problem or constitute a need in the first place. Of course, to meet a need is not the same as preventing it from arising. One could logically ask how God is to meet their needs, if at the same time He is expected to stop or change the events that bring them about. It is a good question, but they will seldom ask it. They must think that when Jesus Christ promised that they would have "trials and tribulations" in the world that He was only kidding around.

Many would not deny it and may not realize themselves that they came to the Enemy's camp primarily as another way to avoid pain and suffering. If an allegiance with God can protect them from "bad things", then why not? Insurance policies can help one deal with bad things when they happen, but an almighty and loving God could prevent their very occurrence in the first place. Besides, He doesn't charge any premiums.

When humans talk about when "bad things happening to good people", they fail to give much thought as to what is really meant by "bad" or who is really "good". Like myself before our time together, they seem to have misread pain and suffering as always being bad things in all cases.

R.J. Aldridge

Of course, most of what they complain about is the result of their living in this marvelous fallen world, where Our Father Below is the primary administrator. They ignore the fact that the majority of the pain and suffering afflicting humanity is really self-inflicted, meaning that they suffer at the hands of other members of mankind. Even when the suffering is not directly caused by another human, people who know of the needs and have the God given resources to do something to ameliorate suffering in others instead choose not to do anything at all. One of the humans said that he "...often wanted to ask God why He doesn't do something about those who suffer". He quit asking, however, in fear that God would someday ask him the same question.

All too often, in those times when the Enemy does allow pain and suffering to occur, there seems to be a grander purpose behind it. For those who don't believe in God, the shaking of their foundations can sometimes serve to get their attention. Jesus said that "not many rich" will enter heaven, for the rich tend to look to their wealth to provide for their current needs and provide for their future comforts. Take away the wealth and they may see their inherent inadequacies in a clearer light.

A man with a happy family will take delight in that family. Let his wife leave him and his children rebel and he may reconsider from whence his happiness arises. I have heard them say that "there are no atheists in foxholes", recognizing that the possibility of imminent death can alter their perceptions of living. Well and good for those in the military fighting in a far-off war someplace, but how does the Enemy get the attention of a young woman just starting college? Perhaps the big C word, "cancer", will do the trick. It is, I grant you, a severe mercy. By allowing physical and mental pains to touch them in this life, He hopes to save from far greater suffering in the next.

The Apostle Paul spoke of the joy of not only sharing in the resurrection of Christ, but also in His suffering as well. How can the blessings be recognized, apart from the trials? How can they grow

The Wormwood Emails

in faith, if they never have needs which require His intervention? If He suffered greatly (and He did), then why should they work so hard to avoid it? Don't they profess that they want to "be like Him"?

I can see now that we must be careful that the pain and suffering we are able to bring to them. We want it to cause them to disbelieve in His existence, without pushing them so far as to have them seek His comfort. Just enough to get them to curse God, without driving them to their knees.

How I wish that the Enemy would fight fairly. I think it very bad form for Him to take one of our most cherished weapons for disturbing the humans and then turn it into their eternal benefit instead. Rather like being shot with our own gun, don't you think?

With Worst Regards,
Wormwood

CHAPTER 17

From: Wormwood <wormwood@gehenna.email>

Sent: Saturday, October 31, 2020 4:47 AM

To: Wart Hog <warthog@gehenna.email>

Subject: Miracles or Fables?

My Dar Wart Hog,

You indicated that your man has some difficulties in believing certain miracles recorded in the Bible. This is a good start at undermining what his heart says to him about the truth of the scriptures, if you can get his head involved in questioning whether it is rational or not to believe as he does.

To begin with, perhaps we should review what a miracle is and what he thinks it is. When he talks about miracles, he is generally thinking about what could more accurately be termed as magic. You know what I mean, something along the line of a Grimm's Fairy Tale. Princes turning into frogs and then back to princes again when properly kissed, rocks and trees turn into animals or wizards and all that sort of thing. What you will note about magic is that what is described will generally violate the rules of nature itself. How often have you seen nature turning pumpkins into coaches and mice into horses?

Unfortunately, the miracles described in the Bible are generally of quite a different type. With few exceptions, they don't describe things that appear to be against nature, but rather repre-

The Wormwood Emails

sent merely a change in timing or intensity in what is very natural indeed. It is not so much that nature is disregarded as it is accelerated or superseded by its Master.

Witness the miracles in the Bible recorded as having been done by the Enemy himself, in the person of Jesus Christ. He started things out by turning water into wine at the wedding in Cana. To do it all at once in the jugs provided is, I grant you, out of the ordinary, but the fact that the Enemy provides the plants, rainfall, soil and sunshine to make millions of jugs of wine every year all over the world gets little attention.

In a similar way, it is said that Jesus fed thousands using no more than a few fish and loaves of bread. The only thing unusual about this is that He chose to do so at a single sitting. Every year, a few fish in any lake or ocean can and will produce many hundreds more. In a similar way, the grain necessary to bake a few loaves of bread, if planted instead in fertile ground, can produce much more grain, enough for many loaves indeed.

Even the miracles of healing are not really outside of the natural scope of things. Most of modern medicine is based not on providing a cure for an illness as to find ways and means to assist the body to heal itself. If there is no life in the body, medicine itself can never help. How fast will a cut on the arm of a corpse scab over and heal up, regardless of how well you stitch, disinfect and bandage it first?

Personally, I think that the miracles recorded for them in the Bible are there for a purpose. Humans are always looking for verification aren't they, that something is true. What greater indication that Christ is God made man that to have him do all of the same kinds of things that the Enemy himself does all the time? Did not Jesus say that he "does only what He sees the Father doing"?

The first thing to accomplish is to keep your man from making any distinction between the miracles of the Bible and what he would expect to read in any fairy tale. You might think this hard

R.J. Aldridge

to do, given the obvious disparities between the two, but it is far easier than you think. He is used to the critics of the Bible declaring it "full of fairy tales". Evidently, he already half believes that himself.

It is also helpful when you can compare the miracles of the Bible, or at least what he thinks they say, with the so called "facts of science". These facts change often, of course, but perhaps he is dense enough to believe that whatever are the current opinions of the scientists are absolute truth, rather than just their latest suppositions.

As an example of how this works, many Christians have a lot of trouble accepting the truth of the Bible and the miracles contained therein based on their understandings of the story of creation. They find the notion quite incredulous that God made the earth and the universe in six quite literal 24 hour days less than 10,000 years ago. In light of the scientific evidences that are stacking up pointing to a very old earth and an even older universe, it isn't any wonder that this is the case. What you must do is try to have him defend the "young earth" idea, in the face of any evidences to the contrary. If he cannot believe it wholeheartedly, he may abandon all of the Bible based upon his difficulties in getting past his concerns about the creation story.

What you must not do is let him in on the fact that there are many, strongly evangelical Christians, who believe that the earth and the universe are actually quite old and that the "days of creation" are in fact, much longer periods of time. As a believer, what really matters after all, is not how long ago the earth was created, but that it was created at all and didn't just come into existence and organize itself on its own accord. If you fail in securing his soul for hell and he ever does get a chance to approach the gates of heaven, entry there is not based on a correct answer as to the age of the earth.

As to miracles, the human Einstein was reported to have said that "There are only two ways to live. One is as though nothing at all

The Wormwood Emails

is a miracle. The other is as if everything is." Obviously, we want your man in the first camp.

With Worst Regards,
Wormwood

CHAPTER 18

From: Wormwood <wormwood@gehenna.email>

Sent: Saturday, December 19, 2020 5:08 AM

To: Wart Hog <warthog@gehenna.email>

Subject: Marriage

My Dear Wart Hog,

So your man has proposed? Marriage can be excellent campaign territory for us but it can also be disastrous if the chosen partner is more dedicated to the Enemy's causes than to her own. I've checked the files and I'm afraid that you've got a problem on your hands.

First the little coffee serving strumpet interested him enough to entice him into joining a Bible believing and teaching church, and now she intends to take him as her spouse as well. I really do wish that we had the freedom to just kill them off when they get so very troublesome to us!

The humans don't seem to fully understand that when they marry, in the eyes of the Enemy and therefore in what constitutes true reality they really do become "one flesh". Not sharing one body, of course, but in some ways the spiritual union is even stronger than a temporary physical one could be. If they marry, you will really be dealing with the two of them at the same time.

If the union is consummated, you must work paw in paw with

86

The Wormwood Emails

her tempter, Magog I believe he is called, from here on out. Every strategy that you employ for capturing the soul of your man must be coordinated with what Magog is employing towards securing the soul of his woman and vice versa. The strategies that you employ must work together or they possibly will not work at all. This is not to imply that the salvation of one is inextricably linked with the other, only that what you do with the one will strongly affect the other.

Even though her files indicate that she is dedicated to the Enemy, all is not lost if she shares the delusion of many human females that marriage will provide for her total personal fulfillment. Christian females are no less immune to this malady than their unsaved sisters. In fact, I sometimes find them more so, as the diverting pursuit of gross materialism is generally of less concern to them.

We are also at an advantage in that the male and female of the species are so radically different in the way that they think about things. Not quite from separate planets, but close enough for our purposes. The female is first and foremost, a "romantic". Never let that out of your mind, Wart Hog! They generally enter a marriage looking for a non-stop continuation of the courtship and the honeymoon and soon find that other things tend to take precedence over the romantic side of life. It is hard for the men to worry about bringing flowers home from work when they are more worried about keeping their jobs and paying the bills.

What the male is about is "achievement". If the mission is to win the female, then he will make every effort to do so. Men, as you should know by now, have very little in the way of true romance in their bones. Most of what they do exhibit, the females have taught to them in one way or another, by virtue of movies they have seen or books they have read and they are to a degree, just playing a part. They are trying to get along in a foreign country, so to speak, but most of them don't really know any Romance languages. Once the wooing is done, he is ready to move on to other,

87

R.J. Aldridge

more natural roles and to new conquests.

This is where our opportunity lies, Wart Hog! The female is likely to judge the quality of the relationship based primarily on what elements of romance, communication and commitment she sees in it. In contrast, the male will make his evaluation based upon the degree to which he is able to provide and to protect. Using different yardsticks, it is no wonder that they reach differing conclusions as to the state of their union.

It should also be noted that marriage is all too often based upon individuals joining because of their weaknesses, rather than their strengths. The quiet man marries the extroverted wife, the spendthrift wife marries the frugal husband, etc. What starts as an attraction based upon a perception that the partner can make up for a shortcoming of their own can easily develop into resentment that the other is so different and that they refuse to reform themselves to suit their mate. The wife above "never stops talking", the husband is "cheap", etc. When this occurs, you have the delightful situation of a marriage in trouble because the people involved are by nature exactly what they were when the initial attraction occurred.

So what is the key to a happy marriage? Since the institution was designed by the Enemy, I should think that His scriptures cover it nicely. The man is to "lay down his life" for his wife and the wife to "love and respect" her husband. The man is called to sacrifice, if necessary, all that he is and hopes to be for the wife and family. To protect and provide, naturally, but perhaps also adding an element of romance whenever possible. After all, to lay down one's life has the connotation of meeting needs too.

The wife is to love and respect her husband. We demons are still a bit in the dark as to what this "love" really means, but I take it that it has in mind putting the other person first. The respect part is obvious and appears to be very important to the human male. Regardless of his occupation and how it may be evaluated by the world at large, he really needs to have his wife feel that he is valuable and significant.

The basis, therefore, appears to be sacrificial giving and unconditional love on the part of both parties. A human didn't get it far wrong when he said that a successful marriage isn't a 50-50 proposition, but one in which both sides give 100% of themselves to the other.

When a marriage is failing, sometimes the humans think that adding a child or two to the equation can somehow strengthen it. Unless they understand the fact that a marriage must be based on the joys of giving to the other party, they are unlikely to find more happiness in the very real demands that come along with children. If either party is still wrapped up in themselves and the pursuit of their own happiness apart from their partner's, they are unlikely to be capable of disinterestedly desiring the happiness of children.

Lastly, remember that chains do not hold a marriage together. It is threads, hundreds and thousands of tiny threads of shared experiences, confidences and memories which sew people together through the years. What appears to be very small things, when taken together, build into a bond far stronger than passion can ever bring about. So if you are going to try to work for their separation, the sooner the better!

With Worst Regards,
Wormwood

CHAPTER 19

From: Wormwood <wormwood@gehenna.email>

Sent: Wednesday, January 13, 2021 10:12 PM

To: Wart Hog <warthog@gehenna.email>

Subject: Prayer

My Dear Wart Hog,

You haven't mentioned your patient's prayer life. I trust that this means that this is an area of no current concern to you. I take it that he follows the routine of most of those who express a belief in the Enemy and even many of those who attend His churches regularly, the "bless me" syndrome, also known as the "never ending shopping list". In most cases, this is a very accurate description of the process.

You know what I mean, when virtually all their prayers are pleas to the Enemy to give them material things, to help them accomplish something which they desire, to protect them from dangers (both real and imagined) or are otherwise and nearly exclusively self-directed. Even on the rare occasions when they try to pray for others, they are likely to pray only for those of their own family, their close friends, et. al. Even when in this circle, they most often are praying that these individuals also contribute to their personal happiness by treating them better or agreeing to something which they themselves may want.

When this type of human prays, they usually begin with a quick

The Wormwood Emails

repetition of words that they think pleases the Enemy, perhaps because they have heard something like them used so often in public prayers. Often you will hear them employing archaic phraseology, perhaps thinking that God hears only the type of English used during the reign of James the First of England.

This is followed as quickly as possible with the real reason for the contact, their list of personal petitions. I sometimes think that these humans conceive of the Power that created and sustains the universe as nothing more than some form of cosmic aide for

self-improvement. If they had the faintest notion of Him, as we cannot avoid, they would treat the whole matter of prayer very differently indeed. Many seem to think that their desires become holy in prayer simply because they ask God to secure them.

You might think that they would follow the example of Jesus himself, who as God and man combined, should have a good handle on the subject of communication between the two. The first thing that they would notice about Jesus was that he treated prayer with great respect and although God himself, showed true reverence for that portion of God which was not with him. Some humans that I have seen are prone to casually flip out prayers like they are joking with their friends, not coming into the presence of the great and awesome I AM.

The other obvious difference is that Jesus spent much more time in prayer than most of the humans would ever consider appropriate. He was known to arise before daybreak or even to pray throughout the night. If Jesus felt prayer so very important, you would think his present day followers would as well. Like the disciples in the garden, however, they too will probably be asleep in minutes.

Why, Jesus even gave them a sample, or format, if you will. Most of them parrot this back, without taking the time to think about what it means or should mean to them when constructing prayers unique to their own situations. I believe that the Lord's Prayer, although not an exact outline of the structure that they should utilize in all circumstances and at all occasions, is a useful technique for them to employ. It begins with recognizing the status of the Enemy as God and offering Him homage as holy and worthy of worship. Then they are to submit to God's sovereignty as in "Thy will be done". Next come the petitions, with an emphasis on needs more than wants and the present more than the future. Dangerous ground follows, when they not only ask for forgiveness for themselves, but also promise to forgive others. Simple and straightforward, to be sure, but there is real power in it. Do try to keep your patient away from anything like this technique for prayer.

The first rule is to help him to assume that any prayers that he would come up with on his own are somehow inferior to those produced by the professionals. This will limit his prayers to selections from a prayer book, regurgitating a minister's words from a Sunday meeting, etc. The farther the prayer can be moved from his own heart, the more likely that it will contain nothing more than parrot talk.

When he does attempt to pray on his own, always keep him focused upon himself. Remind him that he always must be looking out for number one. After all, if he doesn't pray for his own desires, who will do so? Try to make sure that the patient never develops what I call an "attitude of gratitude". A man in such a state will be thankful for and satisfied with virtually everything in his life and therefore much less inclined to make constant demands for more.

Try at all costs to keep the idea out of his head that prayers, when properly focused outwards, can result in a real change in the world in which he lives. All prayer, when done correctly, is a very powerful thing. It certainly is not, as some of them suppose, an old woman's idle amusement. Properly and consistently done, prayer does indeed change things, even things within oneself. If anything, it is the most potent instrument of action available to them.

The Wormwood Emails

I have heard from some of the other tempters that there is a revival stirring in certain Christian circles to reintroduce the practice of fasting with prayer. Why they ever stopped, I don't know, as Jesus clearly taught that fasting and prayer often go hand in hand. If this rumor is true, I shudder to think of what that may accomplish.

The Enemy wants his prayers to be based upon praise, worship, obedience and requests for actions which are commensurate with His own will. We want prayers more like a petulant child asking, no but rather demanding, an increase in his allowance because he somehow thinks he deserves it.

With Worst Regards,
Wormwood

CHAPTER 20

From: Wormwood <wormwood@gehenna.email>

Sent: Friday, March 12, 2021 2:13 AM

To: Wart Hog <warthog@gehenna.email>

Subject: Money and Possessions

My Dear Wart Hog,

You haven't told me anything of substance about your man's feelings about money. You may be familiar with the phrase in the Bible about the "love of money being the root of all evil". Not always that simple, but close enough! Remember also that Jesus had more to say about money and material things than any other single subject. Clearly, He understood how important financial matters would be to them.

The first thing to accomplish is to have him think that all he earns and all he purchases is his own property and he can do whatever he wishes with it. You might think this difficult to accomplish, given the Enemy's teachings that they are no more than "stewards", but it is really quite simple. From the days in the nursery onwards, a very familiar word for him has been "mine".

In point of fact, nothing at all is ultimately "his". The things that he thinks he owns in this world can be taken away through natural disaster, lawsuit, theft, or by virtue of poor investment results or other means. What he has left will remain behind for others, however deserving or undeserving, when he dies.

The Wormwood Emails

As to his body, he can be evicted from it at any time, almost always against his will and certainly with no right of appeal in the matter. He probably also mistakenly thinks that his time is his own. He may feel that he has some kind of a right to a "normal" life of eighty years or more. When you get right down to it though, eternity for them is really just a heartbeat away.

Once he crosses over that line, his body decays and eventually returns to what Genesis calls the "dust of the earth". If the man is a Christian, His eternal soul will be taken by the Enemy, with claims based upon both creation and redemption. If not a

Christian, we make the stronger claim for Our Father Below based upon conquest and the fact that the man is already more like us than like Him. That is to say that the man is a rebel, just like us, refusing to the bitter end to yield himself to the Enemy.

No, nothing at all ever really is ultimately his; except, perhaps, his choice to serve Our Father Below or the Enemy as his master. Ultimately, whether his eternal destiny is heaven or hell is a natural outgrowth of this decision. To choose to belong to God is to choose all that He is and to find that heaven itself flows out of His person and His personality. To choose against God is to opt for Our Father Below, who was the first to make such a choice. I have found that it is possible to define hell as simply where the Enemy isn't!

Regardless of his lack of true ownership, it still helps immensely if you can get him to constantly think of things in the possessive sense. That way, he will then be primarily concerned about doing what he wants with what he sees as his own, rather than trying to please the Enemy through proper management as any good steward should.

If possible, it is often helpful if you can get him to think of money as "bad" in its own right. Many humans misquote the verse that I mentioned above and declare that "money" and not the "love of money", is the root of all evil. Money in and of itself is morally neutral, of course, and is nothing more than a tool which can be

95

used for good or for ill. The same funds that hire a prostitute can be given to the poor to buy food, while money given to the sick for medical care can just as easily be spent on opiate based drugs. It is the attitudes and the actions of the humans that make all the difference, not the money itself.

If he begins to think that money is evil, at least as far as the Enemy is concerned, he will generally feel that the Enemy isn't really interested in it at all as it is but "filthy mammon" to Him. Your man will remain interested in money, of course, and will feel rather guilty about this attraction. Rather than seeking the Enemy's will on how the funds allotted to him should be employed, he will likely hide them away.

Feed his greed, of course, by fueling his desires for more and more. We touched on this theme earlier when we spoke about materialism. He will naturally be looking for happiness in what he can acquire and you never wish to discourage this pursuit. When he doesn't experience the lasting satisfaction that he seeks and which possessions can never really provide, try to persuade him that he needs just a little more money to pull it off.

While we are on the subject, do all that is in your power to get him into debt and then keep him there! I praise whatever fiend in the Infernal Bureaucracy conceived of the idea of credit cards and other such schemes. I can think of no single invention of the modern era that has caused more pain and helped our causes so much as easy credit at high interest rates has done.

A hundred years ago, getting a loan was very difficult for most of the humans on anything other than real estate. Even then, the down payment required was larger and the period allowed in which to pay back the loan much shorter than they are today. What is wonderful is that he can now finance nearly every whim and indulgence. Cars and boats, furniture, vacations, clothes, electronic equipment, etc. The list is limited only by his avarice and the merchant's abilities to put together payment options.

When you combine the strongly materialistic emphasis of

The Wormwood Emails

today's society, his natural greedy tendencies and easy credit, you have a very powerful weapon. Use it fully, Wart Hog and he will be so busy fighting off his creditors that you will have little difficulty in working deeper and more eternal harms on him.

Unless (or until) he destroys his credit rating, he will be bombarded with opportunities at every juncture to go even further into debt. Why, he probably gets nearly ten unsolicited offers each month for one new credit card or another. Try to convince him that he somehow deserves the things that he merely just wants. Paint a rosier picture of his future income than what is maintainable, so that he feels he may be able to support such payment levels. Help him to forget the other financial requirements that he has or is likely to run up against; such as medical bills, car repair or home maintenance needs.

Once you get him heavily into debt, he's as good as ours! He will work ridiculous hours, trying to earn more money to service his debts, putting a strain on his family and social life. He will be more willing to cut corners at work and do unethical things to help him to get ahead. I have had clients who have done things that are clearly illegal when asked to do so by their bosses, since their debt loads and lack of resources to fall back on make them totally fearful of losing their jobs.

He will despair that the financial hole he has dug for himself is far too deep to get out of debt by conventional means, so this will be your opportunity to get him involved in gambling. He can't afford to gamble, of course, because gamblers always end up losing. How do you think they build all of those multi-million dollar casinos, if not on the backs of their losing patrons?

At this point, it won't matter to him, as he will see his only deliverance as being in a big win. He will find himself dreaming constantly about the next big lottery that he is sure to win and what he will do with all the lovely money. Of course, he won't win, which is your cue to assure him that next time he can be the lucky one.

R.J. Aldridge

In the meantime, he is unlikely to cut back spending, obtain counseling or otherwise take constructive action to get out of debt. At home, when he is not fighting with his spouse about money, he will be too tired or ashamed to take time to study the Enemy's scriptures or to pray and meditate on them. On Sunday, he will probably want to skip church entirely, just to get a chance to sleep in. If he does go, he will either give nothing at all or far less than the Enemy's tithe, for he simply can't afford it. The Bible says in Proverbs that "the borrower is servant to the lender". If you get your man to be a servant to enough of them, he will have little time and energy left over to serve the Enemy.

With Worst Regards,
Wormwood

CHAPTER 21

From: Wormwood <wormwood@gehenna.email>

Sent: Friday, March 26, 2021 5:32 AM

To: Wart Hog <warthog@gehenna.email>

Subject: Culture and Pride

My Dear Wart Hog,

When you say that your man is "cultured", what exactly do you mean by this? If you have in mind, as I think you do, that he merely fancies himself to be so, then this is a chink in the armor that we may be able to exploit to our own advantages.

I have found that the motivation behind much of what they call the pursuit of culture is really just common pride dressed up in evening clothes. In an effort to make themselves seem to be more intelligent, more discerning or otherwise superior to their brethren, they embark on the trail of sophistication that they feel such a culture can bestow. This often comes after they have achieved some degree of material success and can financially afford the efforts.

You can often spot these people by virtue of their rather sudden shifts in taste to what is deemed proper by the right set in the world of music, fine art, literature and theatre arts. Please note that what is proper to these folks is seldom what is popular to the masses. It is this pride in being different, in being better and more discerning than their more common neighbors that is the basis of

R.J. Aldridge

this unique form of snobbery.

This is not always the case, as some of them just have a taste in music and the arts which leads them in this direction regardless of what others think about it. As someone once said, "that's why they make thirty-one flavors". Flavors of what, I cannot recall just now.

The humans who pursue art for art's sake are rather easy to spot, as they don't care very much about what others think about anything at all. Such an artist may paint in a certain style because they like to do so, regardless of whether the critics like them or whether they sell anything or not. These are not our quarry. Frankly, they are relatively immune to public opinion and peer pressures, which are just the forces that we like to bring to bear.

What I have in mind are those who are always trying to read the "right books" and attend the "right shows", not so much because they enjoy them, but simply so they can see and be seen and later make clever comments to impress the others. I have known some who have gone to the opera for years, hating (or sleeping through) nearly every performance but enduring the whole thing for the sake of form. Some of them build up a certain endurance for it and come near to an acquired taste, but they never really learn to like opera very much.

If your man is of this type, then by all means pursue culture. With respect to the majority of the people that he meets, his growing belief in his own refinement will make them appear in his eyes to be somewhat less than himself. His circle of peers, "friends" he may even dare to call them, will be the only ones that he feels are his equals. If he ever makes a social faux pas of sufficient magnitude, however, they are likely to drop him like the proverbial hot potato. After all, he will have offended their overly refined sense of propriety. They are willing to spend some time with him now, when he appears to be as perfect as they wish to be. When he falls, they will not likely stoop to help him back up again.

As to his attitude towards God, his pride in his refinement will soon shift to a more general pride in himself and he may even begin to believe that he is truly superior to other, more ordinary human beings. He may, in fact, go so far as to think that he is actually quite special. This is to be encouraged for as you know, people who feel they are quite special, seldom see the need for a Savior.

Pride in any form is a feature that we adore, for it puts distance between the man and others of the human race while simultaneously doing the same between himself and God. Yes, I have found pride to be highly effective insulation material.

So encourage your man to attend events that he doesn't like, read books that he doesn't understand and buy expensive art that looks like the aftermath of a horrendous accident of some sort. Try to get him to think that anything that is popular with the masses is uncultured and therefore is beneath him. Not because it is of inferior quality, of course, but merely because it is popular. If anyone ever assails his opinion as to what constitutes real art, they can be silenced by a few well-chosen epithets; such as "Philistine", "red neck", or "Puritanical".

By the by, if your man is like most, he may feel an occasional pang of charity run through his heart. A feeling that he "really should do something" for mankind. When this arises in him, try to divert his giving to the places that are already feeding his sense of pride. This can usually be done in conjunction with some kind of fund raising efforts that are usually designed to feed the ego. Things such as buying a brick with his name on it for the new theater, being listed on the brass plaque out front or named as a Patron in the program come to mind.

What will ensue is that his charity can be diverted not to the truly needy in this world, but to service the entertainment desires of people such as himself. He will, in fact, be advancing the causes already espoused by his own group, rather than reaching out to those who cannot help themselves. If done correctly, you can turn his gifts to charity into gifts mainly meant to enlarge his

R.J. Aldridge

own sense of self importance.

With Worst Regards,
Wormwood

CHAPTER 22

From: Wormwood <wormwood@gehenna.email>

Sent: Sunday, April 11, 2021 12:50 AM

To: Wart Hog <warthog@gehenna.email>

Subject: Pleasures

My Dear Wart Hog,

In your next email, please tell me something about your man's sense of humor. What does he find amusing? To what does he turn when he is seeking diversion?

I am quite sure that the Enemy does not lack in what the humans would call a sense of humor. Anyone thinking to the contrary hasn't looked at the animals that He created in Australia or sat in any American airport on a Friday afternoon, simply watching the people pass by.

Despite this, I have found from personal experience that the pursuit of amusements and the sub category of humor offer several highly effective ways in which we can make attempts on the human's souls. You will also find the techniques are often effective because they are insidious. Places where he will go to seek amusement are usually far removed from a church building and he will not likely see any connections between the two.

Laughter often accompanies joy, fun, jokes and sarcasm. By all means, we want no part in joy, which seems to be a natural human

R.J. Aldridge

emotion arising principally out of successful interpersonal relationships with family, friends and the like. In a similar vein, fun appears to be something akin to the play instinct of their youth. All too often, it seems to be the vehicle by which joy eventually arrives on the scene. Joy and fun have the same kind of frothiness about them as accompanies much of what they call music. I naturally distrust and consequently dislike them all. Try to keep such frivolities in his life at a bare minimum.

As to jokes, I would say that whether we should encourage them or not depends entirely upon who tells them, the circumstances when they are told and to what end is the central purpose. With the possible exception of jokes that are blatantly sexual, racist or sacrilegious with respect to the Enemy; I find their laughter to be offensive. My experience has been that jokes that are deemed funny by the humans based upon mere incongruities and which lack the elements listed above are too close to fun and do not accomplish our purposes.

Of course, there is something which they call the practical joke which is in reality not a joke at all, but simply cruelty masquerading as humor. This is really very like the fourth area, sarcasm. Hopefully, your man is one of the sarcastic types as mine is. You had said that he seems somewhat intelligent, as far as humans go. Often such intellect, if not channeled into productive service to others will instead turn into a type of weapon of words. When sarcasm is cloaked as just another joke, the damage to another person can be both quick and deep.

What we want, when we have to endure any kind of laughter at all, is laughter that is directed at others. Towards this end, the practical joke as well as the sarcastic witticism can both useful to us. Sticks and stones may break their bones, but broken bones heal. Injuries to the soul can hurt more and sometimes will never completely heal.

I can't locate some of my earlier emails right now, so I cannot recall what we discussed on the subject of pleasure earlier in our

The Wormwood Emails

correspondence. Normally, I take pride in my highly developed sense of procrastination, but I admit to occasional times when it would be better if I finally took the time to get organized. Someday I fear that I'll lose this entire file on the Dark Web without having even backed it up properly.

What I think I said before was that all pleasures are the Enemy's invention. The satisfaction of each of the desires that He has built into them is really His domain and not ours. We have done much to try to invent our own type of pleasures but at this point, all that we can do to produce sin is to induce the humans to take their pleasures at times or in such a way as the Enemy has forbidden.

When a hungry man eats, the satisfaction that he feels is the Enemy's invention and is meant, I believe, to help to maintain human life by making eating pleasurable. The best that we can do is to encourage them to eat far too much, resulting in the sin of gluttony and perhaps negatively impacting their health and lifespan as well. In addition, we can often add the sin of mismanagement of resources, as they spend too much time and money on their own stomachs.

When within the bounds of marriage they seek satisfaction of their sexual urges, they naturally obey the Enemy's edict to "be fruitful and multiply". With some effort, we have taken this very powerful drive within them and twisted it a hundred different

ways. Such sexual perversions as we encourage give them far less satisfaction than what a happy long-term relationship within marriage can provide. Like overeating, promiscuity can add a variety of health risks as well.

Not to belabor the point, but the best we can do with pursuit of pleasures is to try to make them both the means and the end. If they seek sexual, or any other pleasures for their own sake, the experiences give them less and less satisfaction and leave them feeling increasingly empty afterwards.

R.J. Aldridge

I do hope that someday we will have some pleasures to offer that have little or no positive potential. I believe that we are getting quite close with many of the narcotic and psychedelic drugs, not to mention alcoholism. In these, the pleasures would in most other circumstances be deemed anything but pleasurable.

In the meantime, however, get them to focus on happiness, or whatever they mean by that. You may be surprised, but most of them couldn't define the word for you or give you clear cut direction as to how it is to be obtained. Yet in most of the western world, happiness (or at least the pursuit of happiness) is seen as a natural right. In America, they even quote the phrase in their Declaration of Independence and say that the Enemy has ordained it so. While I admit that the Enemy allows them far too much happiness for my tastes, I hardly think that even He considers it their absolute right!

Try to assist him in the pursuit of feelings of pleasure, rather than a state of peace and contentment. If he can be led to confuse the sensory stimulations that are mere byproducts for the genuine article, then you've got him on the treadmill. While he may experience some things which he deems pleasurable at the time, happiness itself will remain elusive. It is rather like confusing the Christmas goose for Christmas itself, I suppose.

Thus, a man that marries and truly attempts to love a woman and the children that their union produces will often find a depth of happiness in that relationship that cannot be experienced in any other place. His bachelor friend that sleeps with far more women, won't ultimately find any lasting satisfaction in having done so with any of them.

From what I have observed, happiness is a natural byproduct which is derived from the pursuit of the Enemy and His ways. It is neither within them or outside of them, but instead is a result of their union with God. Keep them separate, Wart Hog, keep them separate. We can abide an occasional pleasure if we must, but don't give them happiness in the bargain.

With Worst Regards,
Wormwood

CHAPTER 23

From: Wormwood <wormwood@gehenna.email>

Sent: Friday, May 14, 2021 5:01 AM

To: Wart Hog <warthog@gehenna.email>

Subject: Love and Marriage

My Dear Wart Hog,

I am disappointed that you didn't invite me to the wedding. Not that I enjoy the services that much, mind you, but I do so love to throw things at them afterwards. Oh well, perhaps you saved me a piece of the cake?

So, he went ahead and married her, did he? This will make things more difficult for you. Attacks on his chastity will probably be unfruitful, at least for a few years, as he takes delight in his new wife. They have so few possessions that virtually every new acquisition for their home together will bring them great joy.

This makes materialism difficult, as the basic formula there is decreasing marginal utility, a fancy way of saying that the more they have, the less each new thing means to them and therefore, the more they will want. When each purchase brings smaller and smaller increases in the level of total satisfaction, they must buy in volume just to keep up.

I have to admit to being at a bit of a loss as to what advice to give you now. Magog has reported that his woman is a Christian of the

108

The Wormwood Emails

first order. That is to say, she seeks to know God as fully as is possible in this world and to live the kind of life here that is pleasing to Him, before sharing eternity in His heaven. Totally unacceptable, I know, but Magog always was a poor tempter.

I even have heard that she spends several hours each week in true worship and prayer. Not the kind that your man has been reduced to, sitting in the pew and thinking about his afternoon golf game. No, I'm afraid this is the genuine article. In my opinion, they should transfer Magog back to the War and Pestilence Division before it's too late and he muddles up yet another assignment.

Your problem now is that her virtues and her prayers will likely spill over onto him. A strong Christian wife is a very bad thing when you are working on the husband. What is closest and at least for the time being remains the most important thing on earth to him is in a spiritual sense as "one" with the Enemy as your man is "one flesh" with her. I don't like the neighborhood.

If only we understood better what the phenomena which they call love is really all about. On the surface, it appears to be a disinterested putting of the other first, with no thought for what can be gained by doing so. It is impossible by definition, of course, for organisms in competition to act that way in real life but nonetheless, that is what it looks like from a distance.

Perhaps it is just a well camouflaged method to go about getting one's own way by appearing to give in to the other. This I could understand. In fact, I would offer my hearty congratulations on the subtlety of this type of stratagem. Do a few favors, make the other feel guilty enough and then make the demands that they cannot, in good conscience, refuse to someone who has "been so nice to them". To fail to yield just "wouldn't be fair".

If love is just a tradeoff, a "the more I give the more I get" kind of relationship, then you may be able to undermine the relationship by having them try to keep score. When he takes out the trash or gasses up her car, he will think himself entitled to a certain level of reciprocation, a quid pro quo, so to speak. In a similar fashion,

R.J. Aldridge

when she fixes a nice breakfast and does the laundry, she will have similar expectations.

Invariably, each will think that they are racking up quite a positive balance with the other. This is partly because each will assign different values to what they undertake and partly due to selective memories on the part of both parties. The other partner will not be seen to be reciprocating equally and this will result in hurt feelings, disappointments and anger. But of course, how can they keep the score fairly when each is playing with a different score card?

What is so terribly confusing to me is that this isn't what the Enemy seems to have in mind at all when speaking of love. In fact, His love appears seems to be completely unconditional. The most famous of Bible verses, John 3:16, states that "For God so loved the world that He gave His only Son and whosoever believes in Him will inherit everlasting life". It sounds like anyone who wishes to can partake without reservation or condition.

His kind of love also seems to be unilateral as well as unconditional. I know that many Christians believe that they are valuable in the sight of God because He created the first model of a man and a woman in His image. They suppose that this spark of the divine in the is the source of their worth to Him. I don't know that this is the case. If you read the scriptures thoroughly, it seems that the creatures are valuable to God simply because He chooses to love them and to elevate them to that status, not because they are intrinsically lovable things. If anything, such sinful rebels should be unattractive to a holy God.

Strictly speaking, it is His will alone that raises them to the position of adopted sons and daughters. These animals which should remain our playthings and eventual food are elevated by the Enemy to a status higher than ourselves. Further, He promises that they will inherit all as joint heirs with Christ himself. Simply inconceivable!

Getting back to your man, try to keep him as confused about love

The Wormwood Emails

as I am. Let him think that it is just the lust associated with sexual attraction, which will fade in time. When it does, he can think that he has fallen out of love and move on to the next woman.

Added to this, let him think that it is a tradeoff for services rendered as we discussed above. When he keeps that kind of score, it won't be long before he feels short changed and will start to look for another, more equitable, partner.

In reality, it would appear that love is nothing more and nothing less than an act of the will to put the other first, to honor them and to give of oneself, to whatever degree is necessary and for as long as required. Positive emotional feelings may also arise, but that isn't the essence of the activity. To choose to love for the sake of it, appears to be the thing in a nutshell, at least for an unconditional Lover like the Enemy. I think I deal much better with lust.

With Worst Regards,
Wormwood

CHAPTER 24

From: Wormwood <wormwood@gehenna.email>

Sent: Monday, July 12, 2021 10:09 PM

To: Wart Hog <warthog@gehenna.email>

Subject: Violence and the Spirit of the Age

My Dear Wart Hog,

No, when I wrote to you about "culture", I meant plays and the opera and all that kind of thing, not the overall societal environment in which he lives each day. Clearly, this latter type of culture isn't something which he can readily avoid.

As I mentioned earlier, I think that the Bureau of Cultural Affairs is doing an admirable job in undermining North American society. This has benefited us not only in our temptation strategies as they relate to the sexual side of their natures, but also to their violent side as well.

You may have noticed that the Enemy designed them with a capacity for anger. Most of them also have the capacity for violence, when such actions are needed either to defend themselves, or people or things of value. Neither of these is inherently sinful. You may remember that Jesus himself is described as being angry with the money changers in the temple. When He took up a whip and drove them out, He was certainly acting with violence to protect the sanctity of the place. I believe that God designed them with a sense of anger, so that they could experience the

The Wormwood Emails

same kind of righteous indignation that He himself exhibits from time to time.

Over the last sixty years, however, we have largely divorced the emotion of anger from the action of violence. We have also elevated violence itself into something far more frequent and intense than it was ever intended to become. Physical violence against each other was truly meant to be an action of last resort and most common in warfare. We have been able to make it little more than just another form of entertainment.

Of course, they have grown more and more accustomed to the false violence that they see portrayed on the Internet, on television and across their movie screens. They wonder why the younger people are embracing real violence? Part of the reason is that they have grown up with a violence that is almost casual in nature. Another factor is that many of them have come to think of a violent response as the first, not the last, course of action to rely upon. I think that the primary reason is simple desensitization. When you have seen thousands of murders portrayed on television by the time you hit your teenage years, another dead body doesn't affect you much. This is often true even if it is "for real" this time.

Like pornography, the pollution of the culture results in far more damage than they can imagine. It may be that they will turn off their TV sets, but that doesn't mean that their neighbors, or their neighbors' children will do so. Just because they don't watch the shows and films, or play the video games, it doesn't mean that they won't become victims of those that do both.

I find it ironic that in this age of such environmental activism, they insist that clean air and water standards be strictly enforced because after all, everyone must drink and breathe. At the same time, they continue to allow and even to defend the pollution of ideas via the media and their sources of entertainment.

Didn't you mention to me at one point that your man has had a bit of a problem with his temper in the past? If you can somehow get him into the culture of violence, perhaps the next time he loses his temper he will do something much worse than just punching the wall. Remember that those who allow anger to control them are much like those who overindulge in liquor, drugs or other intoxicants. What they are really doing is abdicating their decision making from the rational to the reactionary side of the brain. When you link this lack of reason with an intense and yet casual violent response, you may still be able to wreck his life.

With Worst Regards,
Wormwood

CHAPTER 25

From: Wormwood <wormwood@gehenna.email>

Sent: Saturday, November 27, 2021 12:56 AM

To: Wart Hog <warthog@gehenna.email>

Subject: Goodbye and Good Riddance, You Complete Imbecile

My Dear Wart Hog,

So, he's dead, is he? Rather clever of you to attempt to hide the fact by telling everyone that he simply had gone into politics. Even if this was the case, we would have noticed it eventually.

You really should have let me try to lend you a paw. If you had asked me earlier, perhaps I could have been persuaded into helping to plead your case with your superiors at Low Command. You do have a several things that I covet but much too late now, of course, to strike any such bargains.

I suppose that you find it particularly frustrating that he was a victim of a drive by shooting. Died before he hit the ground, I believe the report said. Poetic justice is it not, when the culture of violence that we so promote works against us like that.

His young wife is deeply depressed no doubt. To be widowed after less than a year of married life is quite a blow. Hopefully Magog will have the foresight to try to twist this to our advantage, at least as it relates to her, her family, friends, etc. Perhaps she will be fool enough to blame God for all this. As if it was Him

R.J. Aldridge

and not some deranged gang member who pulled the trigger.

They obviously don't see death as we do. They may pay lip service to how nice things will be in heaven, but when one of them actually makes the trip sooner than they anticipated, they wail on about the tragedy of it all. Well, for her anyway, it may indeed be such. For him, however, his reward is achieved, and he really is home for good. Beyond our grasp, beyond all sin, beyond all pain, he will bask for all time and beyond time in the peace and delight that only God can provide.

The Enemy always has been one for paradoxes, you know, saying things like "the first shall be last and the last first". Perhaps His greatest paradox is in a death such as this, born as it is into new unending life of a type and quality that neither the humans nor we ourselves can hope to imagine.

As an alumnus, I can assure you that you will find the House of Correction for Incompetent Tempters to be a very interesting place. If they ever let you out and if their pain therapy hasn't completely destroyed your faculties, do write to me again. It pleases me so to know that when compared with such incompetency as you have demonstrated, I look so much the better.

With Worst Regards,
Wormwood

Made in the USA
San Bernardino, CA
01 February 2019